OVER THE RIVER AND THROUGH THE WOODS

Brynna Williamson

Stones in Clay
PUBLISHING

Over the River and Through the Woods
Copyright © 2020 by Brynna Williamson, All rights reserved

This is a work of fiction and any similarities to any person living or dead is purely coincidental, other than those historical persons used for the story. Any details used about them are public domain.

The opinions expressed by the author are not necessarily those of Stones In Clay Publishing.

Stones in Clay Publishing
P.O. Box 1302
Newcastle, Ok 73065

Living stones, being built up as a spiritual house for a holy priesthood, to offer up spiritual sacrifices acceptable to God through Jesus Christ. 1 Peter 2:5,
But we have this treasure in jars of clay, to show that the surpassing power belongs to God and not to us. 2 Corinthians 4:7

Cover Design and Graphics by Mindi Stucks
Book Design by Gary Cooner
Saloon Girl illustration by Katherine Holmes Booth
Published in United States of America
ISBN: 978-1-7337093-2-3
Children's Fiction / Religious / Christian / General
2020.02.15

Stones in Clay
PUBLISHING

My Acknowledgments:

Thank you to **Mama and Daddy**, for their support when I needed it, for their never-ending belief in me, and for all of the time, money and effort they have put into this book! For every email we have crafted and for each trip you found a way to go on.

Gramma and Grampa, thank you for the writing conference you took me on— what a special trip! That made a big difference in my 'writing drive'. For the belief and encouragement you have always shown in me. You always knew I could do this. ☺

To **my siblings**… thank you for your support and understanding when I can hardly give you the time of day because I'm so focused on my writing! You have each been very helpful and insightful. Thank you for convincing me that my book was good even when I wasn't sure, and for laughing at the parts I didn't think were that funny!

Caroline— you have been with me through thick and thin! Thank you for being my soul sister since toddlerhood. I'm glad you're my best friend.

To my doppelganger Brenna, who waved pom-poms over email and who motivated me to meet my deadlines with Jane Eyre quotes. You always know how to make me smile!

Nicole— my thick-as-thieves, mischievous, laughter-filled friend! I'm glad for your friendship and for all the times we've sat next to each other and dreamed of what might be.

Allie, oh my goodness! What a talented artist! I specifically remember how much it meant to me when you drew that horse picture for me. Thank you for the time and effort you put into it!

To **Sarah**— even though you barely missed the deadline for contributing, thank you for your willingness! You have always been a sweet friend to me. Here's to being optimists!

Dr. Cooner— thank you for giving a brand-new author a chance! Thank you for looking past 'the seventeen-year-old' and seeing talent.

To **Eve**. I miss you so much. I wish you could be here to see this! You would have been so excited for me. Thank you for your drawing; I know God let you do it for me! See you in heaven, my friend.

Last but most importantly, to **Jesus**— my God, my Savior, my Father, and my Friend. You are the best thing that ever happened to me! I love You and appreciate the thousands of blessings you have showered upon me. May everything that I do be to Your glory.

"May the grace of the Lord Jesus be with God's holy people." Revelation 22:21

This book has a good ending

This is a tribute to my Grandmother who died of a rare form of cancer in 2017. Every time she picked up a book, she said she wished it would just say on the title page whether or not it had a good ending—then she knew if she would read it or not.

Contents

Welcome to the Darley's

"AAARGH, ME MATEYS, is that land that I see in me one good eye?"

"Aye, I beli've 'tis indeed, Captain Elijah!" I agreed.

"I thought so, first mate, I thought so. We've been on the big blue sea for seven-"

"Ninety-three!" Anne broke in.

"Ninety-three years now," Elijah continued, "And I think it's high time to land. What think ye, fellow pirates?"

We all shouted out agreement, swords raised in the air.

Mother's slight brogue filled the air. "Caroline Elizabeth!"

I sighed and slipped off my 'eye patch,' a rag of leftover fabric Mama gave us to play with. "I'll be back later," I said, dropping my 'sword,' a large stick curved like a scimitar, and trudged home.

Mama scrubbed the clothes on a washboard. When I walked by, she called. "Caroline, you know it's high time you made breakfast. I can't do ev---"

"Yes, I know, Mama. You 'can't do everything around here and I need to hold up my end.' I know." Rolling my eyes, I opened the door, hitting the side of the henhouse, with a satisfying thwack! I put the eggs in my apron pocket and gathered the other ingredients I needed.

Papa built Mama an outdoor oven for times when it was too hot to cook inside. Leaning down, I stoked the fire underneath, making it good and hot.

With all the hard-earned ingredients in the mixing bowl, I plunged my hands into the gooey glob of dough, kneading and mixing with all my might. As my hands fell into the rhythmic motion of mixing, my mind faded out of the dreary world of 1856 Arkansas and into the world I called my own. I could see every familiar detail with exact precision: the color of the chandeliers, the smoothness of the dancing floor, the feel of the smooth silk as it brushed against my legs when I danced. I saw the puffy sleeves and the floor-length gown I designed myself, the green fabric flowing to the floor like a waterfall. I drew a breath of contentment.

A sharp bite on my calf broke the daydream. I rubbed it away with the front of my foot, trying to return to the place where life danced in fullness with the dress and the ball. I tried to picture the dress again.

"Ouch!" I exclaimed. It bit me again, bigger and more fierce. I slapped my leg with my dough-covered hand. The pain grew steadily, itching and burning all the way up my backside. I stood... and screamed.

I was on fire!

Papa yelled and ran towards me. Mama screamed too. Every thought became hyper-focused on the intense, burning pain on my backside. I turned in a circle, trying to slap out the flames. My efforts only ended in more screaming. I couldn't reach the tongues of fire. The flames grew as they attacked my body. I fumbled with the thick button of my skirt, trying to slip out of it. My fingers grew clumsy as panic overtook my senses. I shook in agony as the heat nipped with sharp stabs at my hands. I dropped to the dry ground, trying to stop it. The hungry flames covered me like a million ants tearing chunks of flesh from my legs, my bottom, my back.

My back? My hair...

Cool, parching water swept over my body, quenching the flames. I wept in agony, relief, and mourning as my fingers flew first to my hair... or what was left of it. I fingered the charred stubble of hair remaining on my head. I had always been plain, but now my most beautiful feature burned into nothingness.

My adrenaline was high, but even through the tingling feeling under my blue-tinged skin I felt the swelling, tender blisters. I reached down to touch my arm.

"Man alive," Mama exclaimed.

I saw something I would never forget.

Fire!

Everywhere.

And it was all my fault.

The fire spread to the dry grass surrounding me, crackling and crunching in its destructive path. I watched in horror as the baby leaves of our cotton crop wilted, turned brown and fell off within seconds from the heat. I limped to the bucket, ignoring the throbbing in my legs as much as possible. I half-ran, half-limped to the creek.

My mind exploded in agony. I saw nothing but flashes of light, and my head pounded. I fell to the ground. I touched the back of my legs. I didn't dare look because I smelled the burned flesh. It felt sticky and smelled metallic. Blood!

I forced myself to focus on something else so I wouldn't pass out. I saw something distracting all right, there were flames, everywhere. Destruction seemed to follow the orange light wherever it went. Already flames could be seen through the cracks of the barn walls and the leaves of the trees once so beautiful now floated to the ground like blackened snowflakes.

Mesrour, our horse, neighed and whinnied in panic, his hooves flailing up and down as the fire approached him. He tossed his head and pulled at the reins keeping him tied to the hitching post. Mama ran to help him.

I considered the place where my water was most needed. It would take more than the pitiful bucket I gripped to extinguish the roaring, gigantic tongues of flame enveloping my home.

Mama cried out in relief when John, my brother, rushed out of the house, sooty and coughing. He was balancing our sleepy sister Anne on his shoulders. Eli, my other brother, didn't follow.

The house began to creak, the flames licking the roof.

Mama locked gazes with Papa in silent communication. His eyes widened in sudden understanding of what she was about to do. She ran towards the house.

I heard Papa bellow over the wind. "Emily, stop!"

She plunged inside.

John, Papa and I caught each other's gazes and gathered together silently, stomachs churning. They couldn't die...not like this. Not like this.

Mama disappeared inside, was gone a minute, then Eli came running out. Mama followed close behind. He stopped and threw himself, trembling, into Mama's arms. She kissed the top of his head for a moment before grabbing something to combat the fire. I realized I wasn't breathing and I let out a grateful puff of air.

Papa moved forward to throw water on the house, and we jumped into action. Grabbing different containers, from a bucket to a wheelbarrow to a tin cup, we each fought to put out the flames devouring our house. Crops could be replanted, but we needed a place to live.

I watched with my soot-blackened face and aching, throbbing back as the wooden frame of our family home collapsed.

"Get back!" Papa shouted.

With a lamenting groan, the blackened wood folded in upon itself and, with a mushroom-like cloud of ashes, it fell to the ground. We all froze, staring in shock at the downfall of our home. Our family home for generations past lay decimated. We were now homeless. I stood still, my emotions numb in the knowledge it was my fault. Every single thing our family owned devoured by the hungry flames. The family Bible with generations of history written inside, all our money, all the contents of my hope chest. The only things left clung to our blackened and ashy bodies.

Everything Changes

MY BODY ACHED from constant coughing till well into the next morning.

Anne and Eli wandered around chasing the newly-freed animals, oblivious in their childhood innocence to the full disaster our family faced. Cows mooed in joy as they meandered across their new unlimited borders. I winced as something solid brushed against my leg. My burns were bad, but not as bad as I thought in the heat of the moment. I would survive.

From behind me I heard Mama emit a groan and slump to the ground, her knees buckling beneath her. I saw Papa catch her. He took her limp form to a nearby tree stump. I collapsed behind a piece of brick wall which was all that remained of our barn. With my knees pulled up to my forehead and my hands folded over the tops of my knees, I allowed myself to eavesdrop on Mama and Papa's conversation. After all, as the oldest child I figured it would be helpful to know what was going to happen before the others. I chanced peeking around the corner.

"What are we going to do, Peter?" Mama murmured. Her hands fingered her necklace like they always did when she was nervous. She turned and coughed, doubling over as she spat out the ashes in her lungs. With a shaking hand Papa leaned over and brushed back a loose strand of her greyish-blond hair.

"I don't know," he said. He raked his dirty fingers through his ashy hair, letting out a deep breath.

They sat in silence for several minutes.

"Well, it's clear we can't stay here, at least not the way it is now," Mama said, her hand fluttering around on her lap. A tear danced on the edge of her large, grey eyes, the thick black eyelashes fluttering in the breeze. She wiped it away. The Irish do not shed tears, as Grandfather said.

"Yes," he agreed. He sighed. "We can't stay here," he repeated. His head fell onto his chest and he raked his fingers through his hair again.

"Why don't you just rebuild?" I asked as I stood from behind the wall. I set my hands on my hips and walked over to my parents. Mama lifted an eyebrow at my boldness.

"There's no real effort to building anything. Plus, we won't have to up and abandon our own property," I said.

"No, Caroline," Papa said. "We'd need a place to stay in the meantime, enough wood to start over, help clearing away the burned things, money to buy nails and such with…" He stopped counting the items on his fingers and trailed off as the hopelessness kicked in. "There's just too much. As much as I'd like to find some way, I just don't think we can stay here." He sighed and shook his head. He wiped his sweaty forehead on his shirtsleeve.

"Well, then, what are we going to do? Where can we go? How can we get enough money to survive?" Mama stood up and began pacing.

I took this as my cue to leave them to their own devices. I smirked. *Well, at least to their knowledge, anyway,* I thought. I slunk behind a tree and tried to climb its branches, but was soon cursing my body build I inherited from Papa. My short but strong arms couldn't reach the lowest branch, so I just slumped against the hot bark of the tree, hoping it hid me.

"I don't know what to do now," I heard him reply. "I'll have to get another job somewhere, because a carpenter's salary won't generate enough money to buy new land and build a house while feeding five other people."

"What was saved?" Mama asked after a moment. She turned to face him as I peeked around the corner.

Papa took in a shaky breath as a sudden gust of wind tousled his hair. Today his eyes lacked the sparkle they always held. "Not much, Emily. But I'm thankful we thought to put aside a little money in the bank, though it's not much."

She nodded slowly.

Papa stood, his black-stained face streaked with sweat. "Emily, I'm going into town. Maybe someone can use a hard-working, honest man." He turned with slumped shoulders and limped away in the direction of the town of Clarendon.

I stood and with a sigh I walked into the woods. I needed time to collect myself without the pressure of putting on a brave face for the others. I winced as I lifted my leg over a log. As I approached an oh-so-familiar hollow tree, I crawled through it. I ducked under a hanging vine and climbed over a big hole, dodging by habit everything that needed to be avoided.

I reached my tree, my safe haven. I lifted aside a curtain of leaves and vines to reach the secret room underneath, where previously I spent many hours. I whispered a quick prayer. I didn't want this to be my last time enjoying it. At the base of the ancient tree I settled into the well-worn ridges of the bark, closed my eyes and allowed my muscles to relax.

Something rustled in the bushes. My eyes flew open. I crept as high in the tree as my throbbing leg would allow me to go and snuggled in close, hoping the something would not hear the beating of my heart. I heard horror stories, time and time again, about children who got lost in the woods and never came out. My heart pounded with terror. The longer the thing delayed the more my hands sweat. I tried to wipe them on my skirt but nearly fell, so instead I clutched the suddenly-too-thin bark and prayed I wouldn't fall. With a slight shove of the branches, the thing emerged.

It was Henry "Heart" Williams, my heavyset neighbor. The heart-shaped birthmark on his always-bare foot gave him this name, but woe to anyone who dared to jeer at it.

They would come home with a black eye. I hoped the
rumors I heard about him leaving to get a job in the mines
were true. It would make my life easier.

I loosened my grip on the tree, trying to keep my
breathing regular so he wouldn't notice and make fun of
me.

It didn't work. He pointed up in the tree. "Ah-ha! Found
you, Caroline," he smirked.

My cheeks turned red. I tried to smooth my hair.

He continued, "You look stupid in that tree. Of course,
you look stupid everywhere else, too."

"If I was hiding in a tree, you could bet you wouldn't be
able to find me. Boys are allowed to climb trees and do fun
stuff, but girls should stay in the house and sew or whatever
dumb thing crosses your helpless little minds."

He leaned against my tree and picked his nails. A terrible
smell like rotten onions wafted up from him and I held my
nose, scorning.

"Leave me alone, Heart. I do not want to fight today." I
felt a tear slide down my cheek. I swept it away with an
angry swipe.

"Aww, whatsa mattew? Iz yew feewing too weepy? Po'
Cawowine." He stuck out his bottom lip and batted his
eyelashes.

When he finished his mocking, he threw a stone at me. I
jumped to avoid the rock and swayed on the branch, almost
falling out of the tree. The bottoms of my feet grew
clammy and sweaty, the trademark sign for my dizziness

and fear of heights. When I regained my footing Heart disappeared into the branches.

My face grew hot at his victory since I needed compassion. I should have known better than to expect it from him, of all people. I climbed down from the tree and ran to the place I thought he disappeared. I picked up a sturdy-looking stick. In my haste to show Heart how I was "feewing," I didn't notice the thorn bush in my path. My petticoat, which was my only skirt since the fire, caught in its brambles. As my legs tried to fight the bush and chase after the bully, the sharp thorns poked through the fabric of my skirt and tore a huge gash in the side, revealing a portion of my undergarments. My face flushed as Heart waltzed out from behind a beauty berry bush scoffing at me.

"I'm going to get you back, you bully!" I seethed, shaking my fist while attempting to set myself free.

"Oh, Caroline," he said. He took advantage of the fact I was stuck in the bush. He touched my braid for a moment before giving it a not-too-light tug. I grunted and tried to slap his hand away. "You can't even reach me!" he said as he danced around the edge of my arm's length.

"Not yet, but I will!" I shot back, trying to save my honor.

"Sure, Caroline. Sure." He winked. "Oh, and Caroline — I'll be sure to tell everyone at school about the 'unfortunate' accident with your petticoat."

He made a face as he swaggered away, leaving me without a chance to blow off some steam. I shook my fist at him and with a final tug, untangled myself from the brambles. I retreated back to our land.

I came out from the tree cover and saw Papa running back over the hill, shouting and waving. Mama, who was gulping straight from the bucket of well-water, heard him and dropped it on the ground. We both ran towards him, thrilled to see what he found.

"I — I — he…" he pointed in the direction of Clarendon, heaving and gasping.

"Sit down, Peter! Here, rest for a minute," she soothed.

He took two or three deep breaths before continuing. He explained. "There's a train in Ohio preparing to leave for Alaska. Apparently, there's a rich supply of gold there, with plenty of wood to build something small; not at all like here, where it's too big to cut quick." He slowed his speech and raised his eyes to her, still breathing hard. "That's a good deal, Emily. We can make a living there. It's probably not as cold as they say." He saw the unsure look on her face and pressed ahead, defending his position. "And if we leave right away, there'll still be work left for me to do there. But since we have to leave right away anyway, it's nothing to worry about. And besides, who knows when another job will become available? I think we need to cut our losses and just… go."

The big impact of the little word wrenched my heart.

"I don't know, Peter." She fidgeted with her hands. "Thinking realistically, can we make it all the way there with it being so early in the spring? Especially since —"

He interrupted. "We don't have a choice, Emily. We have nothing to survive on here. No crops, no house, few animals left…"

"But Peter, mining is dangerous! You could be…you could…" she stuttered and looked down at the ground, afraid to finish her sentence. I heard her say, "The Irish are not weak. The Irish do not shed tears. The Irish are never afraid."

He took her chin in his strong hands and gently lifted her face to his. "You don't have to be afraid. God watches over me, and I must take care of our family, no matter the risk."

He leaned forwards and gave her a hug then walked away with his hands in his pockets. Hoping he wouldn't see me, I hugged the brick wall, as he passed on the other side. I saw Mama wiped away the glistening tears from her eyes with the back of her hand, glancing around in either direction. As Papa approached us children we stopped playing and listened to him. We knew the bad news. We no longer have the home we loved. We embraced Papa.

I sat and hugged my knees. I thought about what Papa said to Mama, "Don't be afraid." I needed those words for the next several months.

The next day we prepared to start a different life. No one spoke a word as we abandoned our home. The grey clouds in the sky dropped their tears. The wind tossed the tree branches up and down as if they were waving goodbye to the children who climbed their branches. The air had been washed clean by the rain; it smelled fresh except for the tinge of smoke wafting up from the smoldering ashes of our home.

Papa walked away from his homeland with one, last, drawn-out gaze. The land he had sweat and cried and laughed over. The land he had planned to grow old on. The land he had hoped to deed to us someday. With a sniffle and a dull light in her eyes, Mama walked away from the place of her upbringing, where she had been born. Here Papa had proposed to her, they had held their wedding ceremony, and I was born. This was the place where her grandmother died. Mama blew her nose. John took Anne, crying and clutching her dolly, and lifted her onto his shoulders. He held Eli's hand. Without a word, they walked away. With every one of their hastily-concealed sniffles my guilty heart felt like it had been stuck with a thousand needles. I sagged my shoulders. I made my shoes dusty as I kicked the clods of dirt underfoot.

I shivered in the rain, staring at the burnt ashes which had been my home. As if I might reverse the terrible thing which had fallen upon us. My mind raced trying to think of something, anything, to save our home. I felt this horrible dream would end, and I would wake to the smell of grits and biscuits.

Mama came to check on me. I didn't meet her gaze but remained still, growing angrier at the world. Why did this happen to me? This isn't fair! I don't deserve for this to happen *I'm a good child! In fact, nothing that happens to me is fair! Why don't...*

Just then Mama reached me. She put her hand on my shoulder.

"Caroline," she began.

I couldn't handle any more pity or lectures. "Please, leave me alone!" I cried, running away.

She didn't try to catch me. I passed Papa at the head of our family procession. I almost flew in my haste to stay ahead of everyone and avoid conversation. I wrapped my hands around my wet arms and shivered, my tears invisible as they mixed with the drops of rain running down my face.

That night we slept on the cold, hard ground of the Arkansas prairie. The rain stopped late in the afternoon and made the ground a little softer. Dirtier, but softer. Once I awoke staring straight into a set of animal eyes. My exhausted state kept me from reacting.

The chirping birds woke me. I saw the moon in the night sky. An odd smell of fried fish floated through the air. Although the smell caused my stomach to rumble, I rolled over to go back to sleep when a voice spoke.

"Oh, good, you're up," said Mama.

I forced my heavy eyes open and smacked my lips together. With a groggy-sounding voice, I asked, "What time is it?"

She looked up towards the moon, flipped the meat on the ashes with the end of a stick and answered, "Oh, I'd say about 4:00."

I cried out with full consciousness. "Four o' clock! Why are we up so early? There are no chores to do!" I said. I was not aware I was whining until I came to the end of my sentence.

Mama answered. "You woke up in the early morning so we can get a head start on the day. If you want to complain, you may get up at 3:30, like your father, who caught some fish for us." She gave me a deep stare and raised her eyebrows. "Now, if you'd like to go wash up, the creek's that way." She pointed beyond the trees.

"Yes, ma'am," I mumbled. I stumbled in the direction she pointed. I hated getting up early, especially when I still had several hours to sleep.

As I neared the trees, she yelled after me, "And don't be more than twenty minutes! Breakfast will be ready very soon."

"Yes, ma'am."

I decided not to bathe but dangled my feet in the cool, clear water. Judging by the moon, I sat there for at least forty minutes thinking. I decided I had to go back to our land, even if I rebuilt our house by myself. I would do whatever it took to stay in my home.

Papa came crashing through the trees, calling my name. "Caroline! Can you hear me? I'm coming to find you!" He yelled with a frenzy in his voice.

He stood behind a huge blackberry bush, looking for me. "I'm right here, Papa. What's the matter?"

Papa crouched down and gave me a loving embrace, almost crushing me. "We thought something happened to you! Are you alright?" He stared into my eyes, gripping me by the shoulders.

"Yes, Papa," I said, rolling my eyes. I leaned against his shoulder. "Papa?" I asked as I relaxed.

"Yes?" he said.

"I need…" I hesitated, weighing yet again if I was willing to be separated from my family. I bolstered my courage. "I need to have a talk with you."

"Yes I can! I'm old enough, I'm strong enough, and I have a strong work ethic. Why not? What's the problem?" I challenged.

"You cannot rebuild an entire house by yourself! You are a woman, not a man. Still less, you are a girl, not a woman! Just a strong will isn't enough. You need money, shelter, and food! Where are you going to sleep?" Papa shouted, his arms swinging as he paced back and forth.

"I'll figure it out. Wait! I know! I'll stay with Linda and Nathan Williamson for a while. They will help me. I know it!"

"Caroline Elizabeth Darley, I'm not the kind of father who would intrude on the hospitality of friends!"

"It would just be for a short time! Just until I can save up enough to go out on my own," I pleaded. He shook his head. I broke off a twig and sank to a sitting position drooping my head. Stray hairs tickled my cheeks and lips. "Staying with them gives me a better chance of surviving than coming with you does, anyway," I mumbled, snapping the branch in half. I heard the birds chirping and looked up to find them. I saw Papa staring at me.

"We wouldn't let anything happen to you," he said. His eyebrows were furrowed.

Jumping to my feet I swept out my arms showing the surrounding forest, as I shouted. "Look at us, Father!" I used the title of Father knowing he didn't like it. "We're homeless and in the middle of nowhere with no food, no money, and next-to no clothes! Obviously, the best you can do is not good enough!"

I covered my mouth with my hand as I realized what an ugly, ugly thing came out of it. He frowned at me. His whisper hurt far worse than the shouting he could have used. "How dare you speak to me like that. To me, Caroline." His pained gaze burned me where it touched. My tears were plentiful as my mind raced, wondering what punishment he would dole out to me. But what he said next killed me inside. His eyebrows furrowed as he shook his head. "I am so disappointed in you," he said.

My tears stopped as my shame grew hard like a knob in my throat. I remained rooted to my place, stunned. I had expected a punishment and had instead received an execution.

When the family packed up what little we had, I followed, wordless. I heard my precious Papa say those words once and I was determined I would never hear them again. Once was enough.

I would come.

Our travel over the next two months toward Alaska remained uneventful. On the morning of July twenty-fifth, I

stood, stretched, and ran my fingers through my hair.
Mama was speaking to Eli. "G'morning!" I said cheerily.

"Well, aren't you just a lovely morning person," Eli
grumped.

"Better get used to it, Mr. Bob!" I said, ruffling his hair.
Mr. Bob was the name of his invisible and identical friend
when Eli was little. It was so cute. Sometimes I still called
him Mr. Bob.

He rolled his eyes. Eli cleared his throat as he brought up
the thought on everyone's minds. "Mama, I'm hungry!"

"I know, darling," she said, her eyes downcast. Her
knuckles were white as she gripped them in her lap,
refusing to say more.

Papa came into the clearing, swinging an ax. "As soon as
we find something to eat, we can stop and have lunch," he
said. His smile looked a little too forced to be true. Mama
winced at the reality of his statement.

John stretched and nearly hit me. "Ready?" he asked.

My feet throbbed and I leaned down to rub them. I
heard Mama gasp. A pretty young woman perhaps twenty
years of age peeked out of the forest, her round face
contributing to her young looks. Her long brown hair was
tied back with a handkerchief.

"Howdy," she greeted with a soft voice. She carried a
large picnic basket on her arm. Her plain frock clung to her
back in the heat. "Mah name is Dorothy Coalter. I live just
over yonder…" she pointed to the southeast. "I heard you
say to the younguns that y'all don't have nothing to eat, so
I…" her gaze flickered to the right, her voice trailing off as
she shuffled her feet. "Well, here!" she said with a squeak.

She shoved the basket towards Mama and ran into the forest.

We stared at each other, a little stunned by the oddity of what happened. Eli laughed. "Let's eat!"

Eli reached in and shuffled around a moment before pulling out a hunk of salty cheese. Anne's mouth opened as he handed it to her. He continued to pull out foods we hadn't seen for months: crunchy fried chicken, buttery corn pone, a small pail of milk, Snow White apples, and thick slices of hot bread.

Eli pulled out the last package; the bottom of the basket held no more surprises. We all offered a prayer of thanksgiving for the provisions of our loving God.

Later that day we passed into Wichita Falls, Nebraska. I prayed for the stench rising from the dirty, rodent-infested streets would never burn my nostrils again.

I had goosebumps on my arm as we walked through the eerily quiet town. The wind whistled through the leafless bushes, moaning and wailing. Old buildings loomed above us in silent observation, all of the windows shattered or broken out. Not one bird twittered or chirped, not one squirrel skittered from branch to branch. Red dust whirled around in the wind, coating the yellow grass with a dull layer of dirt. A tumbleweed rolled past us on a long street with abandoned shops. There were rusty knick-knacks and merchandise still in the dark windows. There was movement in one building. I strained my eyes to see one of the worst nightmares of a happy child with a loving family... an orphanage. Standing silent behind the tall iron fence, about fifty scrawny children gathered in groups. They wore identical, long, dress-like pieces of clothing, their faces dirty and thin. We walked past them and noticed their large, hollow eyes watching us. I felt Mama's arm creep over my shoulder with a tight grip. Her other hand went to her necklace and fingered it. The orphans stared at us with the same fear we stared at them. Two boys fought with each other. One appeared to be about fifteen-years-old and the other no more than five years of age. The older one's fist was poised in mid-punch, his knuckles resting on the smaller child's already bruised face. The younger one cowered, not bothering to resist. Another child feasted on ants swarming from an anthill, and yet another nursed a black eye. We continued to stare at each other.

I felt something cold and metal connect with my hand. I shuddered when I saw the giant padlock, on the gate of the orphanage with chains. Mama's fingers went from the necklace on her throat, to hugging us closer. She clutched Eli's hand as he watched the starving children.

"Eli, don't look back. Just keep walking." Mama said to him as her feet pounded the dusty ground and her face was tight.

Anne tugged at Mama's skirt hem. "Mama, I have to go bathroom," she said. She gripped her midsection and jumped up and down, dancing an impatient dance.

"Here?" she demanded.

Anne confessed. "It's an 'mergency. I already went a little."

Mama, who had been struggling to potty-train Anne, licked her lips and scanned the town. She shook her head.

"Anne, not here. We'll stop in just a very few minutes, alright?"

Anne continued hopping. "Oops," she said, frowning. We watched a couple drops of liquid fall to the ground beneath her dress.

Mama grabbed her little hand. "Alright, let's go. Caroline, do you need to come?"

"Yes." I answered falling in step with Mama and Anne.

"We need a necessary," Mama whispered to Papa as we passed; as if someone around would hear her indelicate comment. He nodded in understanding.

We completed our business and headed back to Papa and the boys when the shadows beside us revealed the shape of a man. The darkness wrapped itself around him with his black hair and black eyes as if there was no bottom. He held an iron rod in his hand. His thin frame reminded me of a centipede, twisting and scuttling in an expensive black suit.

"Are these your children?" he demanded in a guttural accent.

Mama tried to hide us with her slender body. Her spidery hands fluttered behind her to keep a grip on each of her children's hands. "Who are you?" she demanded. A breeze blew. "I am Dietrich von Krueger, the orphan manager." He chuckled and hit his rod in his palm several times. I shuddered with each thwack of the rod against his hand. I looked away as he continued. "Excuse me, orphanage manager."

Mama backed away.

He came closer to us and we froze in our tracks. He stopped hitting the rod against his palm but increased his grip on it. "I suggest you answer me."

"Yes! These are my children. Why do you want to know?" Her words flew together, the panic in her voice apparent. She shrunk back. Anne tripped on a large rock, trying to imitate her mother as she walked backwards while keeping her eyes on the man. I swung her onto my back.

"Why do I want to know?" He let out a whispering chuckle. The gravelly sound of his voice gave me the shivers. "I'm always searching for little ones," he said. He flashed a crooked grin, then melded back into the shadows.

We wasted no time in getting back to the boys.

Mama and Papa's eyes met, their conversation both instantaneous and unspoken. They instructed me and John.

"Caroline, take Anne." I shrugged. Already done.

"John... Eli."

John hitched Eli up on his shoulders. We all fled the town. Mama in front, Anne, John, Eli, and me in the middle, and Papa bringing up the rear.

As we prepared for sleep, I considered the day's events. Papa whittled with his pocketknife. The fire's light danced on his bearded face. Eli reclined on Mama's lap, reading his book as she wove a basket made from the sticks she found on our journey. Her hair was mussed and yet she still tried to keep some sense of normalcy in her routine by keeping her hair high behind her head. John and Anne sat on a log ten or fifteen feet away, examining the stars. I heard him point out a constellation to her. We all relaxed around the crackling, popping fire, the crickets chirping and the air growing chilly for the night. The stars shimmered as I lay on the ground. A humid breeze drove through my clothes and I shivered, enjoying the sweet air.

Eli spoke. I watched. "Mama," he said with an earnestness beyond his age.

"Yes, sweetie?" She continued weaving.

"I am desperate for a new book to read. I've read this same one ten times since we left."

She laughed. "Oh, darling, I doubt you're 'desperate' for a new one. But if you find something we can sell in the next town, perhaps you can trade for one."

"No, really! I'm desperate!"

Papa joined in. "Are you positive that's what you meant? Because 'desperate' means willing to do anything in order to get what you want."

Anne climbed into Papa's lap and threw her arms around his neck. "You mean like the babies?" He smiled at her use of the term "babies—" a term she used for any child who was not related to her.

Mama put down her basket-weaving. "Yes. Those children were staring at us because we have things they've never had. We have each other, we have hope, we have love. We were something different from them. They were 'desperate' for good care."

"Let's bring 'em with us!" suggested Anne.

Mama smiled. "It would be wonderful, sweetheart, but I'm afraid I can't take care of that many children at the moment." There was a silence before she continued. She folded her hands in her lap and cleared her throat. "Speaking of… not taking care, I just want you to know…" she trailed off and Papa put a strong hand on her arm. "We just want you to know, no matter what happens on this trip, we will always love you." A pang of anxiety shot through my heart at the mere mention of a possible tragedy. "Of course we know, Mama," replied John. He stood from the ground and put a hand on her arm.

"Yes," I added.

"We love you too, Mama," replied Eli.

Anne hugged Papa tighter. She gave him a big, slobbery kiss---their tradition. He laughed.

Mama changed the tone of the group, speaking in an unnatural cheerful voice which didn't fit the circumstances. She smiled and said, "Alright, time for bed, everyone! Good night, darlings. Sweet dreams." She ran a loving hand over my forehead and leaned down to give me a kiss.

"Good night, Mama," we all replied as we settled down on the ground.

"Good night, Boo," Anne said to me from across the fire.

"Anne, I've told you before please don't call me that!" I rolled over, putting my back to her.

The last thing I remember of that horrible day was Mama's face smiling at me before I drifted off to sleep. Next I knew, I was in a dark alleyway. John and Eli held my hands. Dietrich von Krueger emerged from the shadows, much the same as he had earlier. He carried the same rod of iron. I looked behind him, and saw an army of ragged, pale children behind him. They had large, hollow eyes and reached out to me with a plea for help. They seemed to be mouthing "save me, save me." I stared at them. Von Krueger snatched Eli from my hands and beat him without a sound. I screamed, but no sound emerged.

Mama's hand on my shoulder woke me up. "Caroline, time to get up," she said. I took a deep breath to calm my beating heart from the nightmare.

Oh good. Another day.

I remember the next day more than any other in my life. John and I walked side by side, along the dirt trail, each absorbed in our own thoughts. I glanced up when something small hit me on the head. Another drop of water hit me square in the eye. I rubbed my eye, listening to the pitter-patter of slow rain drops hitting the leaves. We stopped walking for a moment. Papa gauged the speed of the drops and the likelihood of being caught in a storm.

"I'd say little to no chance of getting a rainstorm," Eli said, effecting a very manly-sounding voice.

And then it started pouring.

At first I rushed for cover under a nearby oak. As I stood there, dripping wet and getting wetter, the thunder of the rain drowned out my worries. I stared at Eli and laughed. He stood in the same spot sopping wet, hands on hips and his chin up in a proud swagger. My hair clung to my face in strings as I leaned back against the tree, laughing. Then Anne began to laugh, and then John, and – world of wonders! – even our worn-out parents chuckled.

Eli beckoned to me, releasing his impossible posture. I came a foot closer and gave him a smart-alecky look. He beckoned again, his eyebrows raised and a smile playing in his eyes. I crept closer, but remained ready to retreat at a moment's notice.

About a foot away, he swooped to the ground, caught up a handful of muddy water, and dropped it over my head. I screeched in disbelief, still laughing. I pushed him into the puddle. He pulled me in. John and Anne joined us. A piece of soggy leaf stuck to the top of John's head. We all laughed at him before he pulled it off.

We splashed around in the mud puddle then stood in the rain rinsing ourselves, until the rain slowed to a final halt. The sun speckled through the trees onto the ground, making a slight steam rise from the forest floor.

"Alright, young'uns, time to get a move on," Papa teased.

We gave each other a hand standing up and then re-started our solemn journey. That's not to say we didn't jostle each other and give each other knowing looks. Once in a while I broke out in a giggle.

By the time our clothes were dry, we entered Pawnee City, Nebraska. I stood on a hill, overlooking the people coming and going from the shops. Judging by the size of the town square, the town seemed to be a good size with many people.

I saw a lady come out of a store with a hatbox, a man toting a bag of feed from a general store, a water wheel running a lumber mill, and then... world of wonders, a library. Eli would be so excited. I nudged his shoulder and pointed to the bright building. His eyes widened and he began squirming, itching to go. I smelled candied apples coming from somewhere. Someone had knotted a large banner to the roofs of two buildings. It read "Welcome Home, Sherriff Conway!" in large, friendly, letters.

"Emily, I'm going to the general store to replenish our supply of meat," said Papa. "Why don't you all come?" Mama nodded and stood to her feet with a groan. My knees popped as I stood; a peculiar quirk for a young person like me.

We crossed the dusty street to the general store. The bell over the door dinged as Papa swung it open. "Hello?" he called.

A small man with a long face walked up to the counter. "Can I help you?" he asked.

"Yes sir. I'd like a pound of ham and a pound of salted beef." Anne made big eyes at Papa and he smiled. "And a piece of licorice for each of my children."

"Yes, sir, I'll get that for you," the man said. He went into the back room and returned with the items, which he set on the counter. "That'll be two-ninety-seven, sir," he said.

Papa pulled out a bill and handed it over the counter. The man took it and his face screwed up into a look. "Sir, I'm afraid I can't accept this," he said slowly.

"I'm sorry?"

"I said I'm afraid I can't accept this money, sir," he said.

"You can't accept it?" Papa's tone bordered on upset. "Pardon me, but why not?"

"Yes sir, I'm so sorry. It's just that... well, you see, this money is illegible. "

"The ink ran because we were caught in a rain storm." Papa explained."

The man shook his head.

"I can't accept it," he said.

"But it's good money! It's only wet!" Papa shouted.

The man shrugged in dismissal.

I set down the fabric I was fingering and motioned for the others to do the same. This store didn't want us there.

"I see." Papa turned to leave, his cheeks bright red. Whether out of embarrassment or anger, I wasn't sure.

As we pushed the door open the man spoke. "No, wait." He hesitated and threw a look over his shoulder. "Tell you what. Just this once, I'll take it. I can see when a fellow's in trouble." He smiled and pushed the things toward us. Papa walked back to the counter.

A woman emerged from a doorway behind the counter. She was all done up in a tight dress. It didn't do much for her figure. Her black hair was drawn back into a tight bun. "What's the problem here?" she said with a clipped voice.

"Nothing, Hattie. I'm just selling these people some ham and beef," he said.

"Ah. And are they paying you the full amount?" She sent a tight smile in Papa's direction as she looked him up and down with furrowed eyes.

"Excuse me!" he said. "Just what are you insinuating?"

"Oh, nothing, nothing, I'm sure," she answered with a forced smile. "May I see the money, please?" The man behind the counter hesitated. "Nels, give me the money," she hissed in a whisper.

He handed it to her. Her eyes widened as she stared at the money. She set it on the counter. "You aren't paying with this," she said, pushing it back towards him. She used the tips of her fingers, as if it was too dirty to touch. Papa began to protest but she held up a hand. "You do know this money is illegible? You don't expect us to take this?"

Nels interrupted. "Now, Hattie,"

Papa drew himself to his full height. His voice deepened. "Ma'am. I assure you, upon my honor, the money is legitimate. It is wet from the rain."

"Oh yes, I'm sure. But don't you know your honor is worth nothing here?" She waved the money in his face. His face grew livid with rage. She sent him a pitying look and a pouty face. "Oh, no, I'm sure you weren't counting on this? You know I can't take your word." Papa's face went pale. She flashed another tight-lipped smile as she tore the bills in half. "Since these aren't worth anything now, I'm afraid I'll be having to take that merchandise back," she said. She all but snatched the meat from Papa's hands as he dove for the pieces of money floating to the floor. She returned to the back room, clutching the meat.

The small man shrugged and slipped Anne a piece of licorice. "I'm sorry, folks," he said. "There's not much I--- it's just that—" he shrugged again. "I'm sorry," he said. He followed his wife through the doors. We crossed the road again and sat down on a wooden porch.

Papa turned to Mama with a soul-searching gaze. "So," he said in a murmur. He let out a long sigh.

"So," Mama repeated, her eyes glazed over. Her necklace shifted around on her throat with the movement of her fingers.

"What do you think we should do?"

Silence. She buried her forehead in his broad shoulder without a word. Papa put an arm around her as if to shield her from the world.

We heard a cheer rising from the crowd. A woman rushed past us, running towards an approaching wagon. "Conway!" she shouted. She wore a feather hat and a long, bright red dress. She ran off to join the huge crowd.

A man in the front seat of the wagon held the reigns of two big horses pawing the ground. He came closer to the crowd and raised his hands for silence. After a moment the cheering stopped. Everyone remained quiet as Conway reached behind him in the covered wagon. He tugged at something; raising a fist sized hunk of shimmering gold! The town erupted into cheers and celebrating shouts. Several men threw their hats in the air, shouting yee- haws. The woman who had passed us a moment ago shoved her way before the crowd and, clambering into the wagon seat, embraced the man. The rest of the people took her action as their cue to surround him, still cheering.

"Emily," Papa shouted over the din, "He must have come straight from Alaska with gold. He'll have information on how the gold is holding out there. I'd better go talk to him, see if I can arrange a meeting."

She nodded. Papa and I stood. Pushing his way through the crowd, Papa caught up to the celebrated man. I stayed behind him, sure he would send me back if he knew I was there.

"Excuse me!" Papa yelled.

He tapped Conway, but Conway didn't notice him amongst all the fellow well-wishers crowding his wagon.

"Conway!" he shouted.

Conway looked down at Papa.

"I need to talk to you! Saloon at half-past seven?"

Conway nodded. "Thank you," cried Papa, though he knew Conway was no longer listening, nor could hear him anyway.

He and I stopped fighting the crowd and found our way back to the family.

When Papa left for the meeting, none of us said a word. I sat, my knees crunched up to my chin, lost in thought. Mama pretended to weave her basket, but the worry in her hands betrayed her. Eli and Anne sat in the dust at a distance, amusing themselves. John sat up high in a tree, whittling and thinking.

Papa returned. My siblings were sound asleep, as it had been quite a while since Papa left. In fact, I was rubbing my eyes and fighting slumber too.

"Well?" Mama pried. She set down her basket, which was not one jot more completed than it had been when he left.

Papa shook his head and plumped down on the fallen tree we had used as a fireside bench. He dropped his face in his hands. Papa's odd conduct contradicted the chirping of the crickets and the twinkling stars. Mama put her arm around his shoulder.

"Here, darling, take a bit of cornbread… some food in your stomach will make you feel better, whatever the problem is." She patted him on the shoulder slowly.

"No, Emily, it won't. Save the food. We'll need it later." He thrust the plate of food back into the satchel.

"Peter —!"

"You'll understand in a minute." I took my cue to back away. I feared the news he was about to give us.

He wiped his sweaty face over with an old handkerchief. I heard him take a deep breath before he started his sentence. He looked in Mama's eyes. "I talked to Conway, honey." My stomach curdled. Papa knew Mama didn't like to be called 'honey' and he used the term when the news would be bad. Mama's eyes grew wide. "Peter, don't," she pleaded.

He shushed her and pulled her close to his shoulder. "It's going to be alright," he soothed in a husky voice. He sighed again. "Well, I was right… he did just come from Alaska. He said yes, there's gold left…"

Mama interrupted him. "Why, Peter, that's great news. I think I'll go wash the dishes now." She jumped up and avoided his eyes as she started to walk away.

He shook his head and pulled her back down to a sitting position. She buried her face in his shoulder as if to block out the sound of his next words; the words she knew were coming.

"You didn't let me finish. He said yes, there's gold, but now you lose money getting it."

She nodded. Her fingers crept to her throat.

"You have to own the land you mine on, and pay fees on every piece of gold you find. I already asked Conway how much it would cost. He said he's been trying to get his hands on a halfway-decent piece of land for five years, and because of demand, it's going for $800 an acre."

He took her hand and his next words were gentle and even. "Emily, we don't have much money." He scoffed. "We don't have any money." His volume softened. Mama raised her head to look into Papa's eyes. He cradled her shoulder in his large, well-worn hands and finished his sentence. "Em…" He paused as if to prepare her for his next words. "We're going to need another plan."

She clutched Papa's hands. Her face turned white in proportion to her reddening knuckles. "We don't have time to make another plan. We can't. We've got to go. There's no time. We can't—" she said in a low voice. Tears welled up in her eyes.

He took her hand and began to rub her shoulder. "Calm down, honey. We can do this. We will find a way to settle down."

Mama shook her head, her breath shallow and rapid. "No! Not after all we've put into this." Mama cried.

He took her face in his hands and put his forehead to hers. I heard the murmurs of their whispered conversation. "Emily, this family will be alright. We will make it to the end. I swear to you."

Her hands unclenched and she quivered, nodding unsurely. Her breathing slowed.

Papa's gaze met mine and he beckoned me over. I shook my head.

"Caroline, come here," he said.

I shook my head. I felt the pressure behind my throat, a painful lump behind my voice box, built up. I ran into the forest, desperate to be alone.

I tripped over a log in the dark, stopping my escape. I rocked back and forth on the ground, crying. I jumped up and hit a stick against a tree, splintering it into a thousand pieces. I picked up another and did it again. My rage against our unfair circumstances grew into a shouting match with the forest.

"I never wanted to go on this ridiculous, hopeless trip! Oh! What a fool's errand! I knew I was right in the first place. I just knew it wouldn't work! Nothing ever works for me. Do you hear me? Nothing ever works for me!"

I turned and was stunned to receive a slap. I put my hand to my cheek, my mouth open, and took a step back. My eyes already adjusted to the moonlight and I saw my mother standing in front of me.

"Caroline." She said each syllable with emphasis. "How dare you. How dare you make this about yourself," she seethed. She took another step closer. "Have a little piece of advice: not everything is about you. You are a very small girl in a very big world, and if you complain about your circumstances every time you don't like them, then they will bite you in the rear end as you try to walk away. You will be dragged inside your problems and you will never get out.

"This journey is our chance at survival. We are trying to keep this family alive and you are not being helpful. We need to work together for one goal, not separate! You need to start taking life more seriously, or it will take you. Is that clear?"

I nodded, fighting to hold back my tears. I never saw Mama this angry. Not even when she mentioned Aunt Dawn running away to raise Cousin Oliver by herself. Mama's eyes searched mine.

The rustling bushes of her departure masked the sounds of my emotions breaking free in hot tears running down my face. Mama's words pounded again and again in my head, giving me an actual headache. I threw myself on the green moss and muttered, "I'm not a little girl. I know what I want. I want a home!"

The moon moved over several degrees, and I still sat in the forest. I tried to absorb the peacefulness of the woods while thinking about Mama's words. The sound of crunching leaves caught my attention, but not my gaze. I continued to watch the full moon. Papa sat next to me with a little pop in both of his knees and a slight groan. He didn't say a word for several minutes.

"You know she loves you," he said quietly.

I shrugged.

"She does. Just because someone says something like that doesn't mean they don't love you. In fact, it means they do love you — they love you enough to care."

I nodded. "Sure." Whatever would get him to quit talking about it; I felt the tears threatening me again.

"You know that?"

I shook my head, wiping the edge of my hand against the corner of my tear-filled eye. He put an arm around me. I shrugged it off. I felt a little shock as if it couldn't believe my own outrageous behavior.

The pain of not accepting that particular embrace was one I would remember for the rest of my life.

After I rejected him, Papa went back to camp.

By the time the pink sun began its daily ascension, I had determined I would try a little harder. Whatever it took for them to stop nagging me.

However, fate decreed I would take on much more than my fair share of the work. Much more.

We're On Our Own

WE ENDED UP staying the night in Pawnee City. With no money, no job, and no land, another plan needed to be formed before winter arrived.

"Couldn't we just stay here?" said Elijah. He pondered for a moment. "Never mind— I guess Nebraska dirt is too dry to farm, anyway." He put his head down in Mama's lap and she stroked his curly brown hair.

"Besides, we don't have money to build," replied Papa.

"I wanna live in a cave, wike David n' Gowiath!" Anne squealed. She picked up two sticks and sang while tapping them together.

Mama snorted with laughter. "Not likely," she said. After a moment, she started, "My Cousin Izard lives near here —"

"Not a chance! You remember how much he hates children," said Papa.

"Oh yes." She grimaced. "Never mind, then."

After a short silence I said, "Why can't we go back home?"

Mama and Papa cried, "We've already told you that! Don't ask again!"

"Sorry…"

The midnight silence overtook us and soon I heard Anne's snoring.

"Couldn't we go stay with Great-Grandmother Pamela for a while until Papa can get a job there?" John suggested.

Papa stroked his beard. "Now there's an idea," he said to himself. "I haven't talked to her in years, but…. Hmm."

"I'm sure she'd like to see her grandson and his family, Peter. Don't worry. How far do you suppose it is to her house?"

"Let's see now… she lives near Springfield, Ohio, so that would be about… Gosh, Emily, I don't know. We're in Nebraska now, so that's… ah… ah"

"Seven hundred and twenty miles, not including detours," piped Eli. We all faced him, impressed. He shrugged. "My books taught me," he said. He continued, "We'd have to go south for about forty miles until Fairview, Kansas, and then just straight east for the other 680. That means three and a half months of traveling, assuming we're walking."

Mama nodded. "Alright, that's a long way to walk. Do you all suppose we can make it?" She turned to Papa and searched his eyes. "Do you suppose I can?"

This last statement confused me, but it didn't confuse Papa. He gazed back at her. There was a pause.

"Yes, I do," he answered.

Mama pursed her lips. "Whatever you think, Peter," she said.

Papa slapped his knee as he rose. "It's settled. We're going."

The next morning, we gathered our supplies and started walking. I took a deep breath, enjoying the solitude of my own thoughts. As we walked I heard birds twittering in the trees. I could imagine myself climbing the branches swaying in the wind. I spotted an apple tree and took a detour to pluck a large apple and bite into it with a crunch. It tasted sweet in my mouth and made my fingers sticky. I heard rippling water nearby and saw a creek. A handwritten sign on its banks read, "Wildcat Creek." It was a beautiful day with a bluebird flying over my head, chirping and carrying a wriggling worm to her squeaking newborns. The sun sparkled through the clear sky. I smiled at Mama, my walking partner.

Mama's eyes were glazed over as she stared far ahead. Her fists were clenched at her sides as she marched down the alley. I could tell something was bothering her. Either that or her recent emotional swings were showing themselves again. Concerned, I walked over to Mama and stroked her arm.

"Mama, what's the matter?"

She jumped. "It's… it's the forest. It's too big." She looked away.

I nodded. At Grandfather Hine's funeral she told me how he met a panther in the forest. She said she felt afraid of a forested area in case she met a panther and shared in Grandfather's fate.

"Mama, it'll be fine. Don't think about it; here, just eat an apple. Look around at the beautiful scenery." I tossed her an apple.

She rolled it over again and again in her hand. She lost her grip and it fell to the ground. She left the apple on the ground and her fingers found their way to her throat. She began fingering her necklace in the one place where it was worn.

"Caroline, I want you to have something."

"Alright…" My curiosity was peaked.

Her fingers went to the clasp of her diamond necklace. She unclipped it and placed it around my throat.

"Mama..." I breathed.

"I want you to have this," she said. I caught her hand as it shook. I raised my gaze to look into her eyes.

"Mama, why? This... this is your most treasured possession. Are you sure?"

She frowned. "I don't know why. I just---" She looked away. "Call it a mother's intuition. I want to give this to you."

"We're all going to be fine, Mama. Don't worry." I squeezed her hand and smiled.

She nodded. "I hope so, sweetheart. I hope so." But as I gazed into her eyes, I wondered if she knew something I didn't about the future. I decided to ask again later, when she was not so tense.

My ears perked up at the sound of thrashing in the woods. Out of the corner of my eye, I noticed Papa reaching for his knife, then realizing it burned in the house fire. He bent to pick up a rock and disappeared into the woods.

He shouted from the forest cover. "Emily, can you come help me?" She looked back with hesitation at her group of children. She frowned. I shook my head, "Mama, we'll be fine. No panther will get us," I teased.

She nodded again and started into the forest.

"Em?" Papa asked.

"Coming?" she called to Papa.

She smiled back at me.

I stood in silence. A chill went up my spine for no particular reason. A ghastly, bloodcurdling scream ripped through the air. I ran to Mama's screams. Time slowed down. I felt like I was wading through jelly. I tried to push my way past branches, stumbling on roots and getting stuck in brambles. My heart raced a thousand miles an hour. I heard my breathing echo in my ears as I fought to speed up. A million possibilities raced through my head.

I followed their path and saw them lying on the ground. It seemed like everything was red with blood. Only Papa moved. Something black slunk away into the bushes as we approached. I stopped short. I glanced back at Mama and could not recognize her mauled form. A cold rush tingled throughout my body, shooting through my hands. My stomach rose and I vomited in the bushes.

My siblings caught up with me. Eli locked eyes with me, his face frozen in a wild look. John was breathing heavily. Eli snatched my hands. "Mama," he panted. I blocked his view of the clearing. He didn't need to see her like... like that. He should have the privilege of remembering her as she was.

"Eli---" I started to speak but my voice trembled. No words would form on my lips. He pushed past me and ran into the clearing. I saw him freeze. He crept closer to Mama with light steps, as if being quiet would catch her by surprise. As if his gentility would bring her back. He knelt by her side and took her hand. He stared at her. He fell by her side and rested his head on her shoulder. He cried for his 'mommy' and wept as he embraced her for the last time.

"She knew." John whispered. His face was haggard and pale.

"Bubby...?" Anne whispered. She tried to peek out from behind John. John swung her up and set her on his hip, blocking her view. His gaze locked with mine. We both knew what we would have to do. He led them away. I ran towards Papa, afraid if I slowed down it would waste the one chance to say goodbye.

I fell to my knees by his side.

"Papa…" I whispered, trailing a hand over his arm. I wiped my tears away, leaving a streak of his blood on my face. He couldn't die. Not Papa. Not when I needed him most.

He fumbled for my hand. I thrust it into his. My knuckles were white with the grip of his hand. I was never going to let go. Papa turned and half-smiled. "Your mother…" He was struggling for breath now. "She… never wanted…. to go… into this forest. She knew… what would happen… and I wouldn't listen." He chuckled in between breaths and raised a slow, painful hand to pat mine. "Caroline, pay attention."

My pent-up emotions exploded in a bitter laugh. As if there was a cause in the world that could tear me from his next words.

I leaned closer, trembling. "Sweetheart, I love you. Press on… and take care of your siblings. They will love… you… if you give… them a reason to. Stay off the roads… if you can." He raised a hand to stroke my cheek. "You don't know… how strong… you are," he said. He smiled again and his eyelids fluttered before they closed. They didn't open again.

My eyelids opened as wide as they could go. I refused to believe. I stood and backed away, my mouth open and my hands shaking. I shook my head and looked away. Though I was heartbroken, no sobs came to my mouth. The tears were too many to come. I looked at Eli.

Mama filled his world at the moment. He leaned down and gave her one last gentle kiss, his little body shivering. He leaned back and collapsed, hugging her still body. I laid an understanding hand on the back of his head. I forced myself and Eli to leave Mama's body.

We heard Mesrour's frantic whinnying along with the thunder-like sound of his galloping hooves. I saw John dash through the trees where we left Mesrour harnessed. My stomach tied into knots when I saw John's slouching posture as he came back.

He held up the torn halter of our horse. "Gone," he said simply. He shook his head, his eyes puffy and red-rimmed. The end of the halter was bloody, as if Mesrour had cut himself in his mad escape to flee. Or worse, something bit him. A black tuft of fur stuck to the side, matted in the blood.

"Did Mesrour drop anything?" I asked. He shook his head again. Our horse fled, and took our provisions with him. I pulled up my legs, pushing my knees into my forehead, and wrapped my arms around my shins. We sat in silence shoulder to shoulder. The time passed without measure.

I looked up and realized they were all staring… at me.

"What?" I snapped.

"What now?" asked John. His eyes searched my face.

"I'm sure I don't know! Go ask—" My heart skipped a beat. I was the oldest. It was all up to me. Everything. I buried my head in my knees again.

John took up some of my slack as I began to breathe with effort. My chest felt like it might explode. "Well, let's start with the very basics. We need something to eat."

"Ah…." I drew a blank. "Let's move on. What's after that?" I peeked out to stare at him.

"Something to drink," he coaxed.

"I, ah, I think there's a creek that way," I mumbled. I gestured in the general direction of the creek.

"Alright. I'll take the others and get something to drink. Why don't you stay here a moment?" he suggested.

I buried my face back into my knees, not caring to look, but hearing the sounds of them leaving. The deep, woodsy dirt smell on my dress helped me concentrate on reality. I took a deep breath and tried to concentrate just on breathing. I knew I would have to shoulder much more.

I felt John's muscular hand on my shoulder before I thought they would get back. "Alright, Caroline," he started. "No huge rush, but we've got to find a place to sleep tonight," he said.

I shook my head and opened my mouth to say, "You do it." But as I stared into his firm expression, I saw the face of a hurting little boy, whose parents just died. The realization he was thirteen years old hit me like a toss from a horse. I wiped some of the tears from my face and tried to concentrate on what Papa would do.

"I don't know," I mumbled. It came out too quietly. I cleared my throat and tried again. "I don't know," I repeated. "But we must press on."

My First Taste of Life

I SMELLED BACON and biscuits cooking. Alas, it was a dream. I hadn't eaten in over eighteen hours. My stomach rumbled as I rolled over to go back to sleep.

Eli noticed me roll over. "Oh good, you're awake," he said. "I'm hungry and Anne keeps bothering me."

"That's not true!" Anne yelled. "You took my teddy!"

"Did not!"

"Yes you did!"

"No, I didn't!"

"Stop!" I shouted. My hands covered my ears. "I cannot deal with this right now! Just... go find something to eat. Some berries, I guess. Yes, berries sound good. Go gather some."

They went off into a near clearing, still griping at each other. I watched them go in frustrated silence.

John sat next to me with a little sigh. His knees popped. I smiled half-heartedly.

"Hey," he said.

He drew up his knees and sat with me. "Are you alright?" he continued.

I shrugged. "I guess."

He nodded. "Yeah," he replied quietly. "Me neither."

I fingered my necklace- the last thing I received from my Mama. "It's just... I mean... I don't know." I leaned over and rested my head on his shoulder. He didn't move.

"You do realize we can't be seen," he interjected after a moment.

"What?" I sat up and shook my head.

"If people see us, or we stop for too long, they're going to put us in an orphanage," he said quietly. "They'll separate us."

"No, they wouldn't," I argued. A sick dread hit me as I realized he was right. No self-respecting, good Christian citizen would see four homeless, penniless children wandering the streets without 'rescuing' them.

"So what do you think we need to do?"

He shrugged.

I heard thunder rumble and looked to the skies. The clouds were covering the sun. It looked like it might rain soon. The trees swayed back and forth with the blowing wind.

Anne and Eli tramped back to camp with some berries. "Thanks," I said. I took a heaping handful and shoved all of them into my mouth without a second thought.

"Okay, let's go," I said. I wiped my hands on my skirt and walked across the field. I looked back to ensure they followed me. John stayed with them and helped the little ones make their way past the tall grasses.

We entered a cool, damp forest. I shivered as the light rain began to pitter-patter through the branches. I walked a little faster, hoping to find a near town. I slept in the rain once before, and was not eager to do it again.

I thought of anything else besides Mama and Papa. My mind focused on Great-grandmother Pamela. What was she like? Would she be short and wrinkly, like Mrs. Croft down the street? Perhaps she'd be tall and graceful, like Mrs. Leigh who owns the dress shop. I forced myself to concentrate on the mindless topic.

By the time we reached the end of the forest, the rain beat harder, pounding water over our heads. The needle-like drops cleaned my dirty skin. The wind blew without mercy, blowing our skirts and whipping my hair into my mouth and eyes. I made a "follow me" gesture as I shivered again. I made my way down a tall slope into the town, sliding the whole way in the mud. I glanced at the large town square, but instead beckoned to my siblings to run inside the nearest shop. A small bell dinged as we fell inside, dripping, cold, and tired.

A man came out from the back at the sound of the bell. He was a short, skinny man with no hair except a little dark grey around his ears. He pushed large round glasses closer to his blue eyes, making them appear larger. He looked up and down at us, before he spoke.

"Hello, children! How may I help you?"

My teeth chattered together. "N-n-n-nothing, sir, we just came in to get warm and to get out of the rain, if it's alright with you."

He smiled. "Absolutely! My name is Mr. Dirksen." He held out a well-worn hand and I shook it. He continued speaking. "Say, I was about to eat. Are you hungry?"

I was about to decline when my stomach rumbled loudly. I blushed and smiled. "Yes sir, a little."

He exclaimed, "Say no more. I'll be right back!"

He ducked behind the wall dividing his front parlor from his shop. I turned to John and raised an eyebrow. He shrugged in response.

Mr. Dirksen soon emerged from the curtain, his hands behind his back. "Taa-daa!" he said. He brought out two loaves of bread. Saliva rushed into my mouth at the warm, buttery fresh smell. "Sit, sit!" he said. We all fell to the floor. The bread was gone as soon as he could hand it to us.

"So," he started. "Who are you children? And why are you out in this weather?"

"Wew, my name'th Cawo-wine, and thith is John, and Ewi, and Anne," I said, my mouth stuffed full.

"Where are your parents?"

John and I looked at each other. His head shook. Mr. Dirkson showed us kindness and he knew we were not local, but if he knew we were now helpless orphans with no one to protect us, there was no telling what he would do. I had to come up with an answer quickly. My heart beat faster as I glanced into his eyes. I couldn't read his intent.

I managed to stammer out, "Oh… they're not with us at the moment."

Thankfully, he dropped the subject.

As the rain began to fizzle out, we lay on the sagging wooden floor of Mr. Dirksen's parlor, looking up at the cracked ceiling. I busied myself with watching the progress of a June bug attempting to make its way outside.

I rolled to my side. "Psst! John. Do you think it's stopped enough to go out?"

John looked up from his short nap. He propped himself on his elbow and leaned toward the window for a long moment. He nodded then stood. He woke Eli and Anne.

I poked my head behind the dividing wall as my siblings yawned and stretched behind me. Before speaking I watched Mr. Dirksen work on a large map with gilt edges, gorgeous writing, and charts.

"Oh, that's beautiful," I breathed.

He brightened. "Do you really think so? It's been the result of three months work." With a tender stroke he moved his hand over it. "Anyway. I'm sure there was something else you came in to talk about, child?"

"Yes sir," I replied. "I just wanted to say thank you for having us, and we'll be on our way now."

He put down his compass. "Oh, wait just a moment!"

He dug in a small cabinet under the counter. His fist emerged with a slight tremble. He held a huge roll of cash.

"Look, miss, I don't know why your parents aren't here, but I suspect you children need some help. I want to be the one to do that for you." He stretched his hand toward me, offering me his hard-earned money.

I brushed my fingers over the money, tingling at the touch of so much cash. My mind flashed back to the sagging floors and the cracked ceiling of his parlor. "I thank you, sir, but that money's yours. You worked hard for it, and I'm sure it would be useful to you."

He appeared in front of me, blocking my way to the door. "Miss, I worked hard for this money, but it would be a lot more useful to you than it would be to me. Please, just take it." He extended his hand again.

I turned away as my vision grew blurry with tears. His kindness to a bunch of strange children overwhelmed me.

With a smile he forced the cash into my hand. He nodded as if to reassure me, then wheeled around and walked away. My hand opened almost of its own will. I stared at the hand full of cash. I had never seen so much cash in one place before. This money could take us through the rest of the trip- I didn't have anything to worry about anymore.

I walked through the parlor and out of the shop in a complete daze. My siblings followed behind me.

As soon as we were outside, John asked, "Did he give you money, Caroline?"

"How did you know?"

He smiled. His eyes twinkled. He shrugged.

"Anyway, he said he thought we needed help, so please take it."

"Can I count it, Caroline?" Eli asked, bouncing on his heels.

I opened my mouth to answer him, but stopped when I stared at the town. "World of wonders," I breathed. It was a big town, even bigger than Pawnee City. Right in front of us, there was a large strip of land, long and skinny, which had been outfitted as a park. The heavy limbs of oak trees in the park swayed in the same breeze shaking the long blades of grass. On either side of the park, there were entire rows of businesses: barber's shops, eateries, shops, and several saloons. They even had a library, a water mill, and a church. I had never seen so many buildings in one place.

Eli persuaded the money out of my hands. I was still staring at the square when I heard him squeal.

"Caroline! John! Anne! Quick, come here!" We all crowded around him.

"Boo, I can't see," Anne whined. She tugged at the back of my skirt.

I turned to scold her. "Anne, if I've told you once, I've told you a hundred times! My name is Caroline, not Boo!" I turned back to Eli.

She cowered behind my skirt for a moment before she lost interest and toddled away.

"Mr. Dirksen gave us more a lot more than I expected," he started. My hands began to tingle with excitement.

"Well, how much is it?" I asked.

"Twelve dollars! That's more than twice his week's wages!

"Do you know what we could do with that? Why, we could buy acres of land! We could — we could —" I was rocking up and down in my excitement.

John, sensible as always, interrupted my daydream. "Caroline, let's think ahead here. It doesn't matter what we could do with it, the question is what are we going to do with it?"

I took a deep breath and forced myself to calm down. A brilliant idea formed in my mind and I smirked. "Well, we need to relax. Experts say it is essential to be in good emotional condition before one does hard work."

John looked at me skeptically. "Which experts?" he asked.

"Ah…. You know. Some, ah, smart experts." I cleared my throat and changed the subject. "And to relax," I said, "I think we should go to tonight's fair."

I pointed to the large banner over the saloon, "Seneca town fair tonight! Come one, come all, to see the great wonders of Kansas!" I looked over at Anne and grinned.

"Caroline, we can't spend money at a fair! It's important to have that for later, for medical attention or shelter. Besides, he gave it to us for food!"

"He didn't say what it was for; he just said we needed it! It's very important to have a good attitude before taking on a large project, and… well, this journey is a large project!"

Eli's face brightened as a thought occurred to him. "Besides, John, don't forget what pressure poor Caroline has now." He laid a sympathetic hand on my arm. "Don't forget all the responsibilities she's taking on, John!" he prompted. "She needs a rest." He elbowed me and I made a pouting face on cue.

"But —" John sighed. "Caroline, I cannot fight you both. We can go to the fair."

Eli and I glanced at each other and winked.

The Celebration

I TOOK A DEEP breath of the carnival scented air. Anne bounced at my side, tugging at my skirt. Eli's eyes reflected the flickering lanterns of the vendors as they set up their carts. We walked around, soaking up the smells of the salty, buttery popcorn and the sweet watermelon, hearing the chattering of people crowding in front of their favorite attractions. Everyone talked and socialized with raised voices and bright smiles.

"So. What's the plan?" John asked, analytical as always.

"John, don't be so rigid! Be spontaneous; go out, have some—" My nose caught the scent of something delicious and sweet: caramel. I walked in the direction of the smell, hypnotized by the amazing smell of my favorite dessert. It wasn't my favorite for the taste, which was amazing, but rather for the memories behind it. Distinct memories of Mama and myself in the kitchen with a rolling pin and flour on my nose flashed through my mind. I remembered her smiling as she leaned down and let my toddler self spread some flour on her nose to match mine.

I cleared my throat and wiped my eyes, hoping no one would notice.

"Mmm, candy," Eli cooed. He and the others fell in step with me and we got in the long line to purchase the savory brown squares. My mouth watered as I craned my neck around the multitudes of people to see the brightly-lit cart. Performers in the nearest gazebo started playing energetic music and people danced in the park with laughter.

I noticed Mr. Dirksen come out of his shop, turn around, close the door, and lock it. He wandered off in the direction of the dime museum then disappeared behind its makeshift wooden door. Soon a young man, about fifteen or sixteen years of age and dressed in black, approached the door from the shadows. He waited until a loud cheer erupted, then broke the door. No one heard him for all the noise going on. Within a second, he stepped inside then closed the door again. I gasped. John jumped. "What is it, Caroline?"

I pointed to the shop, filled with the need to move around. "I—he—ah, there's someone—the door—" As I stammered, the boy came out of the shop, holding a large bag. He closed the door, looked both ways, and slunk back into the shadows.

John bit his lip. "I'd better go check it out." He made a move past me.

I grabbed his arm. "John David! You are not going anywhere by yourself with that madman about! Now. I'm the oldest one, so let me handle this."

I made sure John was watching before I wandered to a woman near me and said in an extra loud voice, "Excuse me, madam, but where is the sheriff?"

She looked at me with pursed lips then flipped her hand in the air. With a nasal sounding voice she said, "He's in the saloon." She pointed to a certain building. "Now go away, kid, and don't bother me no more." The crowd of men encircling her laughed. She turned her attention to them.

I furrowed my eyebrows and took a deep breath as I left her. I covered the most ground I could in one stride to head toward the bigger saloon, where the lady had pointed. Once I put some distance between her and myself, I turned around, and stuck out my tongue at her. She didn't notice.

The giant saloon loomed in front of me. The old, rough boards were ready and with splinters for anyone who touched them. I backed straight into a tall, mustachioed, bald man. He was frowning in a most unsociable way.

"What do you want?" he asked gruffly. He crossed his burly arms.

I stuttered, "W-w-why, I just wanted to see the sheriff, sir."

"The sheriff's too busy for the likes of you... little girly." He laughed in my face, his rank breath made a cloud of smoke. He hawked a phlegm wad and spat on the ground.

I gagged, coughed, and waved the cloud of smoke from my face. I put my hands on my hips and in my sternest voice said, "Well, I want to see him anyway! This is a matter of the most importance, and I demand to see the sheriff this very instant!" I stomped my foot.

He stared at me. I chewed my lip, unsure how he would react to my demand. To my dismay, he laughed again, stepped behind the heavy oaken door of the saloon, and slammed it in my face.

"Well! I never!" I exclaimed with a huff.

I faced the crowd with my back to the door. I watched the lady I had spoken to earlier emerge from the crowd and approach the back door of the saloon — a door I hadn't seen before. She opened it and went inside, leaving the men outside.

An idea came to me. I sneaked to the back door and glancing over my shoulder I tiptoed inside. The door squeaked as I edged it closed. I examined the area. I stood in a long, pine-paneled room plastered with mirrors and dripping with the scent of perfume. Loud singing and whistling came from behind the door at the end of the room. Small bright colored garments sat crumpled and discarded on the floor, lying next to shoes with high heels. Makeup bottles of all shapes, colors, and sizes sat open on painted chests of drawers. I wrinkled my nose in disgust.

If this is what it will take to attain justice, so be it. Taking off my old clothes and throwing them to the floor, I reached for the best-fitting costume and tugged the uncouth uniform over my body, complete with the matching feather headpiece. I transferred the remaining money from Mr. Dirksen to the small pouch on the side of my costume. I looked at myself in the mirror and my eyes widened. I tried to take a deep breath but found it impossible due to the tightness of the outfit. The dress changed my childish pudginess into a curviness. My hand trembled as I reached for a bottle of make-up on a nearby tabletop.

I heard Mama's warning voice but convinced myself the look would not be complete without all the accessories. I removed the cap and put a little on my hand; it left a soft, red mark. I tried putting it on my cheeks. It didn't look good. It didn't work on my lips either. I tried my eyelids. That worked. The color contrasted with my cloudy grey eyes and transformed them into a glorious green. I twisted my hair into a high braid and pinned it in place. The heels were the last accessory I would need to complete the outfit. I stood, hand on hips, debating with myself. They were so... so garish. I heard Mama's voice in my head again, scolding that I should not even think of wearing them. I took a deep breath. Mama would have realized it's for the greater good. With a grimace, I sat and shoved the hard edges of the heeled shoes around my feet, wobbling as I attempted to stand. I was ready. I nodded to myself and marched as best I could towards the loud sounds.

The chaos coming from that room blew me away. A dancing girl on the other side of the room gave a drawn-out kiss to a huge, dingy cowboy. I viewed the other side of the room, crinkling my nose. In a dark, unused corner, four men played a game of poker. I noticed one of the men, the one closest to me, pull a card out of his sleeve and set it on the table. Eight men were at the counter drinking. Five of them were talking to dancing girls, and the other three looked as if they wished they were. In the front, two men were arguing. They fought with each other, punching and kicking and yelling all at the same time. No one seemed to notice over the sound of a piano man playing a tune with gusto, hurting my ears. A girl sat on his piano. At various tables, men were slumped over table tops, their alcohol mugs clenched tightly in their hands. The bartender, standing in the front corner behind the bar, wiped glasses clean and took drinks for himself; wipe one, drink one.

That's when the smell hit me. The air was saturated with the stench of dirt, the salty odor of sweat, a sweet but fermented smell which I assumed was whiskey, the metallic scent of gunpowder, and the smothering stink of cigarette smoke. I started to reel, dizzy and gagging with the overwhelming reek. My stomach rumbled in protest. I considered walking out and forgetting about the sheriff — after all, what was it to me if someone else got robbed? But no; I felt an obligation to help Mr. Dirksen, since he helped us. I steeled myself and walked off the stage where I entered, still trying to keep my balance. Speed walking in the heels with discomfort, I strolled past the girl and the cowboy, who were still kissing. I walked up to the drunk bartender.

"Excuse me," I yelled.

He didn't turn around.

"Excuse me!"

He rotated toward me in slow motion. His eyes were glazed over as he began to drawl, "Well, howdy there, Candi. Give me some sugar," he leered. I jerked away.

"I'm not Candi!" My fingers were in my ears. I heard a gun go off behind me and I ducked.

"How's the kid, Candi?"

I leaned forward over the sticky counter and slapped him to get his attention. His eyes widened and he jumped back. I tried to shake off the sting in my hand which left the flaming red spot on his face. Though he would slap me back if sober, the drink confused his senses enough to make him take my hit.

"Where is the sheriff?" I asked him, stressing every word.

"Over there, with his wife," he said, pointing. He cradled his cheek but looked more confused than angry.

I followed his point. It led straight to the grungy cowboy and the dancing girl. My shocked gaze followed as the woman left to go backstage.

I raised my eyebrows, doubtful. I went through this for the help of this... this irresponsible, unrespectable-looking cowhand? I shook my head, unsure. I marched in his direction. Something was better than nothing.

I approached him. He went from table to table stealing the drunken men's drinks right out of their hand. Swallowing in one gigantic gulp what would take most men at least five drinks to finish. He was younger than I thought he would be.

"Excuse me, sir," I began.

He spun around, his hat following from its string around his neck. "Well, well, well. What do we have here?" He took an inspecting circle around me. I squirmed under the scrutiny of the outfit I'm sure would make Mama turn over in her grave. If she had one.

After what seemed like forever, he came back around to my front, his hands clasped behind his back. He smiled an impish grin and leaned in close; much too close for comfort. He stared in my face. I could feel his hot breath in to my ear as he spoke in a whisper. I flinched. "You," he whispered, "are rather ugly." The men who had stopped playing cards laughed and cheered him on. Some clinked their glasses together.

I snorted, and moved away. "Well! You're not the prettiest rose in the bouquet yourself!"

My voice sounded weak and childish in comparison to his loud, droning drawl. He looked in my face and laughed. My nerves prickled. I was about to say something else when his enormous size struck me. I hesitated for a moment before I spoke. "Now, putting that aside, I need your help. Someone is being robbed!" No one reacted.

He walked over to another table, his badge flapping against his dirty leather chaps. He took another drink and proceeded to gulp it down, not answering at all. I stood, waiting, right next to him.

"Well?" I cried.

"What do I care?" He sat down at the poker table. He talked to the men playing.

I stamped over to him.

"'What do you care?' How could you say that? You're the sheriff! A poor old man is getting robbed out of his wits, and you don't even care?"

He didn't even look my way before replying.

"Nope."

I stepped in between him and the man to whom he was offering poker advice. "Look, I need your help and I intend to get it. Either you help me, or…" I searched for a sufficient threat. "Or I'll tell everyone that you are a crooked man!"

He grinned and pinched my cheek. "Well, isn't Little Missy here gettin' saucy?"

All the men laughed. My cheeks burned as I stomped my foot. "I —" I started to insist but was interrupted by the boy with the club foot walking in.

Everyone cheered as he entered holding a bag of money and Mr. Dirksen's map. The one he worked on for months. This money and map was Mr. Dirksen's source of income.

"There he is! The thief!" I began to say. However, I was cut off by the young man himself.

"We've got money for a night on the town, brother!" he shouted.

"Ah, I can't wait," the sheriff replied. "Ready to play cards?"

"Sure am! I don't know for how long, though, he didn't have much." He laughed as he stepped down the stairs into the main seating area.

"Something is better than nothing," the sheriff echoed in a twisted version of my own thoughts moments ago.

"He's your brother?" I cried. "The town's own sheriff, a criminal!" I threw up my hands and rolled my eyes. "'If the light within you is darkness, how great is that darkness!'" I quoted from the biblical book of Matthew. I faced the sheriff's brother. "You terrible man!" I tried to slap him, but he caught my arm and started to squeeze. I applied pressure with my foot to persuade him to let go. "Just you come back here!" he threatened, jumping up and down and holding his hurt appendage.

"Don't you threaten me!" I shouted. Panic made my mind race.

I backed away as he approached me. I bumped into the sheriff himself. He restrained me as I struggled, pinning my arms to my side.

With a deep growl, he bellowed, "You insult me, dare to threaten me, and then hurt my brother? Just once I'll let you off with a warning, because you're a woman." I felt like I had shrunk down to about an inch tall. He continued as he pointed to the door. "Now get out before I change my mind and you get worse."

He gave me a shove in the direction of the door. I fell over the steps and landed sprawled on the ground face first. My feather topper fell unheeded upon the ground. His shadow loomed over me as the giant reached into the pouch on my costume, where I stored the money, and he took it. I rolled over on the stairs so I could see him.

"That's mine!" I shouted. I tried to stand up, but struggled because of the slim heels of my shoes.

"No, now it's mine! After all, you wouldn't deny me pay for helping you catch a thief?"

The excuse for a sheriff pointed to his brother, who was leaning against the bar and grinning as he drank. "You done got me, Jack," he said with a mock whine as he held up his hands.

The entire bar roared with laughter and the sheriff held a fistful of my money above his head. I managed to stand, my cheeks burning.

"You are a horrible man," I said, my chest heaving with emotion, "and I'm going to tell everyone what a crook you are!" I snatched the bag of money from the shocked traitor.

I kicked off my shoes so I could run faster around the muscled guard, out the open door, and back into the crowd outside. The stinging tears running down my rouged cheeks made the faces I passed all blur together.

And so I had my first taste of the real world, and I did not like it. Not much of the world was as nice as the kind old cartographer. As it was, how could I make it past this one town; let alone the entire country?

Betrayed

I TORE INTO the crowd, my cheeks a fiery red and my eyes likewise as I rubbed my tears and the makeup all over my face. With my hair still done up in a braid around my head and my petite costume clinging to me in discomfort, I stopped running a moment and felt eyes staring. *I must look a sight*, I reflected with embarrassment. I tried to raise my voice, shouting out what I threatened to, but it came out as a squeak because I was panting and crying too hard. I decided against the breath waster.

The sheriff was following on my heels, shouting, "Stop that girl!"

I dodged the arms of those trying to stop me and ducked under the animal tent, pushing past people. In the brief time I was in there, I heard whinnying, snorting, roaring, bleating, grunting, and angry shouting. I ran out the other side. I darted between vendor's carts and shoved my way through the dancing couples, making the musicians jumble up their music and several young ladies fall to the ground, looking after me angrily.

Far from the saloon, I searched but didn't see the sheriff following me. I released a breath of relief.

My next step was to find my siblings and return the money stolen from Mr. Dirksen. In vain I looked both directions for my siblings. They were nowhere to be found. I rubbed my temples, trying to remember where I last saw them. I walked backwards in time to… ah-ha! The caramel. I walked that direction, being careful to avoid the people I knocked over during my escape. By the time I picked my way over to them, John was in the process of handing over all of our money. I smacked his hand, making him jump.

"John," I cried, "you know how much we need that money! Don't you DARE spend it on such frivolities!"

"Caroline," he protested.

He noticed my peculiar attire. His mouth flew open. I grabbed his arm and dragged him out of the line. The man selling the caramel and most of the line stood still, staring at us.

"Caroline!" he hissed. "What are you wearing? You know Mama and Papa would die of shame if they saw you wear that!" His face darkened.

I sighed impatiently. "I will explain later."

Out of the corner of my eye, I noticed movement. The sheriff and his brother were looking for me. The former began talking to someone in the caramel line, and the man pointed in our direction.

"Right now, run!" I shouted.

"Stop! thief!" the sheriff cried, pointing at me.

John and I took off running, Elijah trying to keep up and Anne toddling behind.

John swung her up on his shoulders, puffing. "Caroline," he gasped as he ran, "Just... what... did you get yourself into?"

I ran faster, but was not going far for the density of the crowd. I ducked inside the dime museum. Someone caught my arm. He pulled me to a short stop.

"Please," I begged, trying to pull away, "let me go! That man is not who you think he is —"

I looked up at my captor and stopped speaking. Mr. Dirksen winked back at me.

"I've got her!" he yelled.

The sheriff caught up, his brother close behind.

"Thank you, Horace. I can take it from here," he said. He reached out and took my arm.

Mr. Dirksen yanked my arm away from the grip of the sheriff. "Tell you what, Jack. I know I owe you a favor, so I'm going to make it up to you. I know you have the jail cell full with Mrs. Dirksen right now, so I will take this child," he tugged my arm in mock cruelty, "back to my house until the morning, when my wife is released. Then you can take her and put her in jail."

The sheriff glared at him. "What makes you think I would agree to that?"

Mr. Dirksen shrugged. "Well, if both women are in there, you'll have the state sheriff after you for crowding prisoners again. After all, that cell measures six by five." Jack's face screwed up in thought. Mr. Dirksen added hurriedly, "And besides, the more people are in there, the more money you'll have to spend to feed them."

The last point won him over. "All right, Horace, but if you try anything tricky —"

"I get the picture, Jack." Mr. Dirksen's grip tightened slightly, but to anyone who wasn't looking close he seemed calm.

He walked away before 'Jack' could say any more.

Once we were behind the crowd and safe from the prying eyes of Jack, Mr. Dirksen let go of my arm.

"Are you alright?" he asked.

I nodded. "I'm alright." I rubbed my arm where his grip had gotten somewhat tight. I looked up at him curiously. "But why didn't you let me run when the sheriff was looking for me?"

"You wouldn't have gotten far anyway. You may as well have been stopped by someone who will help you rather than someone who would have handed you over."

"Ah, good point…" Then I remembered why I wanted the sheriff in the first place. "Mr. Dirksen, your shop —"

He interrupted me. "I know, don't worry, it happens all the time." He started walking. I followed, trying to keep pace.

"But it was —"

Again he interrupted, holding up his hand. "I know: the sheriff's brother. And in case you're wondering, my wife is in prison for standing up to him about it, so that's why I'm not doing anything about it. They have robbed me blind

again and again, and there's not a thing I can do about it."
His hand clenched into a fist. His face turned cherry red.

I ran back to John, Eli, and Anne lagging behind us.
"Are you three alright?"

They nodded, still breathing hard. "Caroline, just tell me;
what's going on?" John begged.

"Shh, don't worry about it now. I'll explain later," I said.
John's sigh in the background ran past my ears as I turned.

As I walked back to Mr. Dirksen, I noticed a tall man
with his back to me finish a conversation with Mr. Dirksen
and slink into the crowd. Our friendly mapmaker took a
deep sigh and shook his head. I caught up to his side,
clearing my throat nervously.

After several minutes of walking towards the shop, I
brought up an important question. "Mr. Dirksen, how are
we going to get out of here?"

"Out of where?" he asked tiredly. He didn't seem to be
paying me full attention.

"Out of town, of course," I said.

He shrugged. "Well, you'll have to give me a while to
think it over. Come back with me to the house for the night
and you can sleep in the parlor."

His eyes looked away from mine.

"It's just... are you sure it's safe to wait to leave?"

"I don't see why not!" The words tumbled out of his
mouth, almost of their own accord. As if he was rushing to
say it.

"Well, the sheriff is expecting us to be handed over to
him in the morning..."

His eyes glazed over for a moment. He turned to me. "Oh, I apologize. What did you say?"

"I said, you did just tell the sheriff you'd hand me over to him in the morning, so I'm just checking..."

"Aw, that." He waved his hand and chuckled nervously.

"Well?"

"It's fine. I won't hand you over." He glanced at me from the corner of his eyes and smiled. His gaze rushed back to the ground.

"Well, maybe we can just leave before morning and be on our way to Ohio!" I suggested.

As I spoke, we entered his shop. It was torn up with the robbery, and as we walked past the public space into the back part of the store, we saw his home was torn up as well. He saw the destruction and shook his head.

"I... I'm afraid that plan won't work..." he said.

A tall shadow flickered behind the closed curtains. On the other side of the room, something enormous twitched. A hinge squeaked.

"W-why not?" I asked nervously, looking around. I already knew the answer to my question.

"Because no one gets out of the hands of Jack Wilder. NO one." The sheriff stepped out of the shadows and flourished his badge. "Now, in the name of the law, I arrest you for theft, assault, and attempted slander of an official...namely, me." A wicked grin grew on his face, and he spat a wad of tobacco on the floor. Mr. Dirksen cringed. The sheriff stepped forward. His broad hand took my arm, gripping it so hard it turned white and I screamed with pain.

Dirksen turned to me with a hollowness in his eyes. "I'm sorry," he said, "he told me he'd hurt my wife and you if I didn't do it this way. I... I didn't want to. I'm sorry it had to be this way." He started to turn away.

"Please, no!" I pleaded.

He didn't answer. He froze.

I turned my attention to the man now gripping my arm like it was pinched in a door. "Why not just arrest me out there when you had the chance?" I hissed.

"Because I knew you'd make a scene, and I need all the public support I can get what with the election coming up," he replied. He shrugged and spat again. "Get the others. We have work to do tonight," he announced. The four younger men who came with him moved to take my younger siblings. The brief thought raced through my mind; I had not been able to protect them for even one day.

Anne screamed so loud the windows trembled. The boy from earlier in the bar slapped her. "Now, now! Let's have none of that," he whispered, leaning down to look into her eyes. I strained against him who held me in place but found myself unable to move. Anne whimpered and trembled, cradling her cheek where it was now red.

I took up where Anne had left off and began screaming for help.

"Stop screaming or it'll get worse for you and your siblings."

He pointed to Anne's captor, giving him the signal to make good on that threat. Her eyes bulged as he started to constrict her middle. I closed my mouth and he let go of his tight grip on her.

"Jack, you said you wouldn't hurt them," protested Mr. Dirksen, holding up his hands in a 'time-out' gesture.

"'Wouldn't hurt them? Wouldn't *hurt* them?" he repeated. He threw a glance at his friends. "Boys, did you hear that? Horace here is afraid we're going to hurt them!" The men all laughed and jeered. The sheriff turned back to Mr. Dirksen. "Goodness, Horace, haven't you ever heard of disciplining a bad child now and then? Why, it's good for them, Horace!" He shook Eli, who was in his other hand, rattling him around.

"Stop that, Jack!"

A cruel light shone from Jack's eyes. "Or what?" He sneered.

A silence fell over the room.

My hopes rose. He was going to stand up for us. We were saved!

Instead Mr. Dirksen walked away.

Jack laughed as Mr. Dirksen left the room. "All alone now, aren't you, little dears? Left all alone with nice Uncle Wilder," he said, shaking Eli with every word. "Poor dears have no one left to help them," he said with mock pity. His friends laughed.

I saw a shadow play on the wall in front of us. There was something behind us. I braced myself for another attack.

The sound of wood hitting flesh echoed in the room. "Ah!" the sheriff yelled. He ducked and swung to the side. Horace stood behind us with a block of wood, heaving.

"Let...go...of...those...children," he said, his face livid.

"How dare you, you little…" The sheriff changed his mind and rather snapped his fingers in Horace's direction. One of the boys walked over, all too easily. He knew Mr. Dirksen could never outrun him. He grabbed the shoulders of our only hope and threw him onto the floor.

"What do you think you're doing, Horace? You weren't going to help, were you? Remember, you have to abide by our deal so I can give you your share of the money." Jack sneered. He turned back to me and continued. "Tell you what. In spite of your outrageous behavior tonight, I will guarantee you your safety, and I'll return 10 per cent of Horace's money to him — all in exchange for this one little, tiny, insignificant necklace." He smirked. "Isn't that generous of me?"

He lifted Mama's diamond necklace off my chest, his grimy hands fingering the last and most precious reminder I had of her. I twisted around and managed to slap him. In a slow and threatening manner, he drew himself up and took a deep breath without reacting. An immediate reaction at least would have been more predictable, but now I had no idea what he was going to do next. I held my breath. He came down and stared into my eyes, unblinking. His soulless black eyes did not move but seemed to cut into my gaze.

"I will give you one last chance; take it or leave it." He added, "And trust me; this is your very last chance." I was dying to look away but not willing to let him think I was that weak.

I opened my mouth, intending to reply, but then couldn't finish.

My eyes teared up. "I-I can't give it to you," I whispered.

"Alright, take 'em!" he shouted, straightening up.

We all began to struggle against our captors, Mr. Dirksen included.

As Anne fought tooth and nail, scratching, biting, kicking, screaming, and wriggling, she dropped her precious dolly.

"My dolly!" she cried. She stopped fighting to reach for it. Her keeper took opportunity to catch her up in his arms. She wriggled against him, but to no avail. He, breathing hard, laughed as he stomped on it. "Stop it! Stop it! You're hurting her!" Anne screamed. Eli lunged in her direction and made it out of his captor's arms before he was restrained again.

I caught John's actions out of the corner of my eye as he let loose a fury I never knew he contained. I never realized how much muscle his wiry frame held until he needed it. In one swift movement, he twisted around and connected his fist with his kidnapper's stomach with a sickening *thwack* and the two began to fight. Before long, his opponent was on the floor, knocked out cold and with a big black eye. In a split second before someone else came to fight him, he rushed over to the sheriff, who was holding me.

"Let go of her," he threatened in a deep voice. In an instant I realized John was becoming a man. He already sounded like it.

The sheriff's mellow laugh sounded. "Or else what?" he joked. He scowled monstrously.

John showed him what. With a flash faster than lightning, he punched Jack in the face so hard his eye began to turn purple immediately. Jack howled with pain, dropped his hold on my arms, and staggered toward my brother.

"Caroline, go!" John shouted. I hesitated between helping him and taking the others and getting out.

That one second of hesitation cost everything. They caught me again and threw me backwards and I went flailing, my arms out and straining to get my balance.

I saw Jack reach into his back pocket and pull out a knife. His hand was behind his back. John would never see it in time.

"No!" I screamed. Jack dropped the knife in surprise.

John's eyes shot up for one second as he looked for me. Always the protective brother. The sheriff took advantage of his inattention in one infinitesimal second. He punched John in the face and then took him in a restraining hold. He started beating on his head. John was moaning.

"Stop it, stop it! You can have the necklace! Take it, just stop," I begged.

The noise in the room ceased. The people were quiet. My interruption had, at least momentarily, distracted the Goliath of a sheriff. He dropped John, groaning, onto the floor. John crumpled up in a ball.

"I knew you would come around," Jack purred, the skin around his eye already an ugly green and purple. He was breathing hard.

I wanted to vomit at the mock gentleness this beast was capable of right after such a violent display. His eyes narrowed and his lips parted to show yellow teeth. He held out his grimy hand and I unclasped the crystal-clear jewel from around my neck, fighting back tears. I thought of Mama as I placed it into his impatient paw. I had to look away.

"Ha!" he crooned with glee. "Boys, do you know what this means? Why, we could sell this necklace and make ourselves rich!" His goons cheered.

The crooked sheriff leaned down to the waking mapmaker.

"I think this means you've forfeited your share of the proceeds from the necklace, Horace." He clicked his tongue. The sound made me shiver. Goose pimples raised up on my arms. Mr. Dirksen opened his eyes for a second. He moaned. "I want nothing else to do with this. You've had all the co-operation you're going to get from me." He closed his eyes again.

Jack laughed and dangled the map over Mr. Dirksen's nose. "Your loss! Tell you what; since I'm in such a good mood, and since I don't need it anymore anyway, I'll throw in this worthless piece of paper." He smirked as a thought occurred to him. "Maybe this will help remind you of what a favor you've done me. Nice doing business with you, Horace!" He laughed and threw the map over his shoulder as he left, making a loud *thump!* It unrolled itself as it hit the floor.

The giant began to walk out the door. However, after a moment's thought, he came back and spat on the map sprawled out on the floor. It was of Ohio.

The downstairs bell rang in an ironically pleasant tone as the sheriff and his family left. Anne picked up her slightly-crumpled but otherwise unharmed doll and snuggled it close to her. John sat up, panting. His cheek was flaming red and he had a black eye. "Caroline, I believe you owe me an explanation now," he gasped. I opened my mouth to answer when his hands flew to his temples and he groaned.

I came up to him and cradled his face between my hands. "Oh, John! Oh, oh…" I searched his eyes and his head. "Are you alright?"

"Yes, I'm fine, just —" he winced as I brushed my fingers over his swollen eye. "sore," he finished. "But oh, my head!" He pressed his palms to his temples.

Dirksen also sat up, wincing. "That was Jack Wilder, the county sheriff, and his boys. You children got him pretty mad pretty fast. He gave you 'special' attention."

"What a privilege," I retorted. I continued checking the younger ones for injuries.

"You must have hit a nerve," Mr. Dirksen added.

John's injuries had turned his normal docile attitude into a sarcastic one.

"I'll tell *you* whose nerves have been hit," he said, trailing off into silence. He peered into the dust-covered mirror and assessed his facial wounds. "Caroline, what did you do to make him so upset?" He stared at me and crossed his arms. Again I reminded myself he was younger than me, not the other way around.

I wrung my hands. "Well, I may have insulted him."

"You insulted a man twice your size?" He glowered at me.

I bit my lip and nodded hesitantly. "Twice. And I also hurt his brother, and threatened him."

"You know that's really not wise," he mumbled.

"Mr. Dirksen, are you alright?"

"Yes, I'm fine. I am so sorry about all of this. I had no idea he would resort to… to…" He trailed off. He looked at each one of us, staring each in the face. He must have seen our injuries, both inside and out. No amount of apologizing and backpedaling would excuse the injustice he had committed against four, innocent, unsuspecting children. He stood there looking awkward. He scratched the back of his head. Then, with one graceful move, he leaned down to the floor and picked up the map. Rolling it back up and rubbing off the saliva quickly, he thrust it out to me without even looking me in the eyes. I took it from his grasp and he tramped back into the back room, offering no more excuses for what he knew was an inexcusable action.

I shook my head. We turned to leave. It was time to get out of this town as quick as we could. As we passed through the hallway to the front door, I noticed a pair of old, leather shoes near my size sitting outside of one of the doors. I picked them up, then tucked them in the crook of my arm. Though I knew I would regret taking something without asking, at the time I figured he owed me at least that much.

We made our way through the shattered glass, ripped up chairs, wood splinters from the table, and wallpaper shreds to the door.

As we walked past the dissipating crowd, John broke the quiet of the moment. "Oh, my head!" he yelled. He clutched his temples and bent over in pain.

"John, don't yell. It'll make your headache worse!" I urged as I stuffed my feet into the shoes.

He grimaced in response.

So as the stars shimmered in the dark sky, we left the borders of what I thought must be the worst part of the trip. It wasn't. Not by a long shot.

Blow to the Head

JOHN AND I studied the map late the next night, as we lay around the fire.

"Here's the Ohio River, so we've got to go up from there…" He traced his finger up towards where Springfield should be. "Ah-ha! There it is." The fire provided light to see where he was tapping. "I think we need to go through Missouri, Illinois, and Indiana before we get to the edge of Ohio."

"Alright." I sighed and rolled onto my back, staring at the sky as I gestured with my hands. "But where does she live in Springfield? It's around a forest somewhere. And, what are we going to do once we get there?" I scoffed. "Rather, 'if' we get there." I sighed again. "Mama and Papa never told me what to do after that." I crushed a lump of dirt between my fingers and studied his bruised face in the light of the dancing fire.

He shrugged. "I don't know where she lives. I suppose we'll just have to ask around, explore a little, hope and pray. That is, unless you have any other ideas. As for what we'll do after we find her—" he shrugged again. "Well, let's deal with one catastrophic event at a time."

I shook my head. "I don't have any better ideas. But however we get there, we need to make sure we stay off the roads as much as possible. Remember what Papa said about four children roaming the country alone…"

John nodded. "True. Some good-meaning soul might take us and put us into 'homes.'"

"Separate homes," Eli added darkly.

Anne interrupted with a wail. She rolled around whimpering, and crying. I ran to her and cradled her small body in my arms.

"Anne, Anne — wake up." I stroked her hair. "It's just a nightmare, Anne."

She opened her eyes sleepily. With a violent suddenness, she threw her arms around my neck. "Boo, I'm scared," she whispered. Her dolly was pressed in between our two bodies.

I ignored the little flip my heart did at the not-so-repulsive nickname and continued stroking her hair. I tried to form my words like Mama would have. "It's alright, Anne honey. You're safe now." My gut twisted as I realized it may not be true. I swallowed my guilt at a promise I could not keep. "Would it help to tell me what your dream was about?"

"No!" She buried her wet face in my shoulder. She spoke again with a muffled voice. "Sing to me. Please?" She gazed into my eyes with her large blue ones.

I stared into those big, round, helpless eyes and found myself singing in an instant. It was an old Irish Lullaby Mama used to sing to me as I rocked on her knee and fell asleep to the warm light of the fire. The memory made me smile as I stroked Anne's hair and embraced her in my arms, rocking back and forth on the ground singing.

The music of the fairy
And of the peaceful sleep,
Every golden Irish evening
Will lull you off to sleep.

The twinkling of the daisies,
The secrets that they keep -
The breeze among the branches,
Will lull you off to sleep.

The laughter of the leprechauns
Is dancing, like their feet;
The rolling, merry melody
Will lull you off to sleep.

May sleep come easy,
My dear, sweet Grah Mo Chree,
For no matter what will happen,
Heaven shineth down on thee.

By the end of my melody, Anne was fast asleep. I laid her on the ground. My eyelids felt very heavy and I lay down next to her.

A purple shadow flitted across my vision. Everything seemed to be moving in slow motion. Someone was singing with an eerie high-pitched voice. I couldn't see anything correctly; the world in front of me was fuzzy. Someone spoke to me, but for some reason I didn't want to hear what they said even though I sensed it was important, I wouldn't listen. I felt as light as a feather. I began to rise, floating up and up and up, higher and higher, now in the stars. I looked below myself and saw the sleeping forms of Mama, Papa, and John, all slumbering in one spot. They looked peaceful. With a start, I realized they spoke to me, but I didn't listen while still on the ground. I yelled for someone to take me back down, but no one would help me. The floating, transparent things next to me took shape and became people, people crying and yelling and straining to reach the people who appeared next to my family on the ground. I continued begging them to help me, but no one was listening. The lights went out and I could no longer see anything. With a scream I woke, feeling chilled in the warm night air. I mopped my forehead and realized I poured sweat. My scream still played itself in my alert mind. The terror felt out of place in the quiet and still night air.

I looked at John, the still form of his fading self in my dream still vivid in my mind. His eyes were closed, regardless of my scream, and his chest rose and fell. In the sounds of the summer night I discerned his gentle snore. He stopped snoring, smacked his lips together, rolled over, and resumed his snuffling snort. I chuckled with a nervous twitter, reassured of his safety. I lay back down and went to sleep. I would not have slept so peacefully if I had noticed John's look of agony as he rolled over.

The next morning, the sky looked like it could rain. I tuned in to the things going on around me. Anne and Eli were still asleep.

"Good morning," I muttered to no one in particular.

I didn't see John. Intense flashbacks from my dream rushed through my mind and I panicked.

"Eli!" He didn't answer. "Elijah! Where is John?"

He opened his eyes and moaned, "What?"

"Where is John?"

He rolled over and closed his eyes. "Leeme 'lone," he mumbled.

He started to snore again. I took a shaky breath and jumped to my feet, adrenaline coursing through my body.

"I need to find him, Eli. I'm going off to look for him. You stay here and watch Anne."

With an innocent gleam in her tired eyes, Anne rubbed her eye with a fist and asked, "Whatsa matter, Boo?"

I sighed. "Please don't call me that. Anyway, I don't want to tell you what's the matter just yet. I… I'm sure it's nothing. You stay here and try to find some breakfast."

I ran off into the woods, the most likely place he would go. *Or the most likely direction for something to have taken him.* With this thought I ran faster. I stopped as I approached the trees and noticed a footprint in the spongy moss. I walked ahead, searching for more footprints, and heard a crashing sound in front of me. My thoughts were full of hungry bears and starved wolves as I hid in a nearby ditch alongside the path. The noise came closer and closer, its cause seeming bigger and bigger as my panic increased.

But then John popped through the bushes, holding two dead rabbits by the feet and whistling. I jumped up from the ditch, grabbed him by the collar, and gave him a sound lecture. The poor boy never even knew what hit him.

"John David Darley! How could you just up and leave us all like that? We're all fit to catch something with all the worrying we've done about you!" I figured the use of the word "we" was close enough to the truth to use it.

He tried to protest. "But Caroline —"

"Don't 'but Caroline' me! What if something had happened to you? What if you had gotten lost or hurt trying to do something by yourself? What then? I'll bet you didn't even consider telling someone where you were going, did you?" I glared at him.

"Caroline, I did tell someone where I was going," he said with an extreme calm.

I felt a blush creep up my face. "Oh. You did?" I sunk off my tiptoes.

"Yes, I did. Eli was awake when I left at 4 o'clock this morning to get some breakfast. I thought I might get a little something to thank you for all you've done for us so far. I told him to let you know when you awoke."

I bit my lip. I stepped forward and threw my arms around his neck. "Oh, John, I'm sorry. I just—I had a dream last night, and… well, I was just so worried about you!"

He patted me on the shoulder. I didn't notice him wince at my touch. He unwrapped my arms from his neck and put them at my sides.

"That's alright, Caroline. But next time, at least give me the benefit of the doubt!" He winked.

I gave him a big bear hug.

The salty-smelling rabbit meat sizzled over the fire, which I made with tedious action of rubbing two sticks together. The four of us sat in a circle and talked.

"O.K. First of all, we need to decide what we're going to do. Mama and Papa wanted us to go to Great-Grandmother Pamela; do we all agree that's what we need to do, at least for their sake?" We all nodded in unison. "All right, then." I brought out the map, tracing our proposed route with my finger. "I think this would be the best way to get there. Does anyone have a better idea?" No one replied. "Elijah? Anne?" They both replied in the negative, and since John was the one who suggested the path, I didn't ask him. "Alright. Should be easy enough. It's not even that far." I forced a smile. "Third on our list of problems are supplies. We need food enough to last us at least three months, maybe a new set of clothes, and a weapon to get food with. Ideas, please?"

"Today I learned to hunt by just waiting and blending in, then catching the rabbits with my hands once they get close enough. If I'm lucky, I can keep doing that."

I shook my head. "But what if you don't get lucky," I stated. "I'd much rather purchase or fashion a weapon, whichever is more practical."

"Well, how much money do we have left?" Eli asked.

I took the money out of my pocket and counted it. "One dollar and thirty-three cents," I announced.

There was silence as everyone took in this overwhelming fact. "Caroline, I think a new set of clothes for you is quite high on the list of priorities," John pointed out.

I looked down at my outfit. In my haste to get out of Seneca, I had forgotten to go back and get my clothes; I was still wearing the sequined, tight dress of a dancing girl.

"Yes, I suppose you're right." It was not the most comfortable outfit. Plus, as it got colder, this little bit of fabric would not be enough to warm me. "Did anyone see a sign in Seneca for the nearest town where we could get these supplies?"

No one did. I inhaled a deep breath and fell on my back. "Okay.... so how could we find the nearest town?"

"Maybe there's someone nearby who will show us," said Eli.

"Look around, Eli. There's no one here."

"Alright, alright! I'm just suggesting," he retorted.

"Yeah, well, next time think before you speak," I said, frustrated.

"Caroline, Eli," intervened John.

"Fine. We'll check around after we eat," I sighed.

"Speaking of which, I think it's ready!" John replied.

We all jumped at the cooked food and tore into the hot, juicy meat. My stomach rumbled happily. It was delicious. With full bellies, we all smiled at each other.

After covering the fire with dirt, we commenced looking for a friendly family who would be willing to help us out. For four hours we searched for any kind of a dwelling, but to no avail. John and Anne were plowing ahead to see what they could find.

With a shout, John came leaping back up the path. "Caroline, there's someone up there!"

He wheeled around and ran back up the path. Eli and I broke into a run. He threw me a silent but pointed look, referencing our argument about someone living close by. I ignored it.

Within two minutes we were in front of a charming stone cottage housed in a blossoming glen. The door was an inviting green and the mossy roof screamed comfort. The long, lush grass beckoned to me, begging for me to take a nap in its cool, refreshing blanket. Daisies, bluebells, rose-of-Sharon bushes, sunflowers and roses decorated the front of this adorable little house. There was a lazy column of smoke protruding from the old chimney, and a delicious smell of baking cookies came from the open windows. I breathed deeply, sauntered up to the door on the winding brick pathway, and knocked. With a delightful squeak, the green door opened.

The attractive lady who answered the door cocked her head. "Why, what are you children doing so far out in the forest?"

"We were wondering if you could direct us to the nearest town," I replied. I noticed her eyes flick over my peculiar outfit once, but she was nice enough not to look over it again.

"But of course!" She looked at the younger ones. "You all look so hungry! Come right in." When I tried to protest, she directed me inside with a hand on my back. "Come, come, come," the lady invited.

She bade us be seated on her beautiful chairs. "Well! Good morning; I'm Rachel Faith!" she declared. She leaned across the table and pumped my hand.

"Hello, Miss Faith!" I replied.

"Oh, no. Faith is my middle name. Cormier is my last name. But you can just call me Rachel." She smiled a deep, dimpled smile. "What are your names? Oh, wait! I almost forgot!"

We all looked at each other, bemused by her forgetful but charming attitude. She flounced back into the room holding a plateful of rather awful-looking, burnt apple turnovers and a jug of milk. She placed both in front of us. I grimaced at the blackened section of pastry, greasy clumps of sugar clinging to the top.

"I was afraid I'd have to eat these myself," she said, smiling. "Have one, won't you?" She picked one up and munched on it, not caring about their blackened state.

Eli looked at me out of the corner of his eye, wondering if he had to take one. I nodded ever so slightly. He took the smallest one and began to gnaw on it.

"How are they?" she asked.

Eli's face went blank. "Ah," he started, floundering.

"Never tasted anything like them, have you?" She closed her eyes as if to enjoy them better.

He plastered a pained smile on his face and nodded in forced agreement. I ducked my head, trying to hold back a laugh.

Dimples came out on her cheek and her eyes twinkled. She shook the red-orange bangs out of her face. "Here, everyone take one!" She passed around the plate and we each took one, trying to look appreciative. I ate mine quickly to get it over with.

Rachel put her chin in her hands and stared at me. "So! What are your names?" she asked.

"I'm Caroline, this is my brother John, this is my brother Eli, and this is my sister Anne."

"Anne with an 'e'," Anne piped up.

"I'll be sure to remember that," Rachel cooed, delighted by this adorable exclamation. "What are you young ones doing all the way out here by your lonesome selves?" she inquired, staring deep into my eyes again.

There was just something about her; I poured out our story.

"…and so here we are!" I finished.

She wiped her moist eyes and took in a ragged breath. "That is amazing. The fact you young ones did all that by yourselves —! And you didn't have anybody to watch over you! It's just too much!" She shook her head making her long red braid fly in the air. "Anything I can do to help, I will do."

"Well, I do need a new dress, so if you happen to have an old one…" I suggested.

She jumped up and grabbed my arm. "Of course! I was about to suggest it myself!"

Rachel led me to her room, chattering about nothing in particular. She closed the door behind her, surveying me. She bit her lip, causing an adorable dimple in her left cheek. "Now, let's see. You and I are about the same size, don't you think?"

I blushed and shrugged. She was much slimmer and taller than I, but I was not about to point that out.

"About," I said. She threw open her wooden wardrobe, bringing out a very well made cotton dress, a light blue thing with no patterns or frills. It looked very sensible. She also brought out a sturdy pair of shoes, which I accepted with gratitude and put on my aching feet since the leather ones, which I regretted taking from Mrs. Dirksen, were much too small. She thrust the garment in my direction.

"Try this one," she suggested.

I pulled it over my head and tried to get it over my shoulders, but to no avail. It was too small. "Ah, I don't think so," I said.

"Well, lucky for you I have one other one!" she said with a cheery note in her voice. She brought a lovely green dress from the closet. Her hands supported it at the top and at the bottom as she laid it on the bed. "Lovely, isn't it," she said.

I nodded.

"Hold it up to you!" she said.

"Oh, no, I couldn't —" I started.

"No, no, it's yours. I insist. Now, hold it up!" she prodded.

I conceded.

"And look! It has a secret pocket sewn into the skirt!" she continued. "Thought of that myself."

"Are you sure, Miss Cormier?" I amended my statement. "Rachel, I mean?" She winked.

"Yes, I'm sure. I probably wouldn't ever wear it anyway," she answered.

I smiled and nodded gratefully.

It was a little long for me, since she was taller than I. I reveled in the touch of the soft fabric and turned to look in the mirror. I gasped. The hemming in the sleeves had caused them to be a bit puffy; the dark-green floor-length dress was my dream dress! I closed my eyes and danced around the room, still holding it up to myself over my outfit.

I faded back into my dream world, where I whirled around to the violinist's waltz in the arms of a prince. The large marble ballroom echoed with the sounds of whispering and giggling, glass cups clinking. The click of the ladies' high-heeled shoes added another sound to the music floating in the air. Dukes and ladies stood on the sidelines, munching on exotic treats. I heard Rachel giggle in the background. Her laughter sounded like bells chiming in the distance.

Suddenly, with a loud thump, someone screamed. The grand ball faded from my view; the bright colors and noises of the dance turned grey and withered, tapering off into reality. I dropped the dress on the floor and flung open the door, darting into the main room. My heart was in my constricting throat.

John lay sprawled out on the floor, his eyes closed and his chair lying on its back several feet away. Anne and Eli were huddled around him. John was not moving.

I fell next to him on my knees. "John! Are you alright? What happened?" He didn't answer. I turned to Eli and grabbed his shoulders. "What happened?" I searched his eyes frantically.

"I don't know! He was fine — just sitting there and talking — and then he screamed, slumped over, and fell on the ground!"

I turned to the still form of my brother and dropped my head onto his chest, feeling for breath. Feeling none, I begin to panic. But I shoved down my fright and calmed my nerves. If he was still alive, perhaps I could save him. I steadied my voice.

"John, stay with me. If you can hear me, do something." *Please, John, please! Move, groan, blink, whatever, but tell me somehow that you're alive!*

A part of me wondered if there might be something harmful in the turnovers, but I had eaten them too and I wasn't feeling sick so I dismissed the thought. I blinked, which caused tears to pour out of my eyes. John still did not answer or move.

Everyone stood over John's body in silence. I longed for some noise. Rachel stood over me.

After much too long, John whimpered and moved his fingers. I felt overjoyed and relieved.

I spoke to him. "It's alright, John. We're going to figure this out. You'll be fine, okay?" *You have to be fine. I need you. Don't you leave me, too.*

He opened his eyes and cleared his throat gently. "No, Caroline, I don't think I will."

I found it difficult to speak over the knot in my throat. "Yes, you are! It'll be —"

He cut me off, raising his hand for silence. "Don't interrupt me — I don't know how long I can wait."

My breathing felt erratic. "John, I can't lose you! I just can't! Not after Mama and Papa." I fell over his torso and embraced him. "And because it would be my fault if you died." His shirt grew wet with my tears.

"Caroline, it wouldn't be your fault in the slightest."

"Yes it would! Since I'm supposed to be in charge it's my fault if you die. And I'm the one who screamed and distracted you and let the sheriff hit you in the eye... Oh, John, it's all my fault." I hugged him.

"Now, Caroline, you know good and well it isn't either. Even if you had told me not to fight for you, you know I would've. Besides, the blow to the head is what did it, not the eye." He forced a weak smile as he touched my face. Heavy tears fell down my cheek, even though I tried to suppress it for his sake.

Eli broke in. "Does it hurt much, John?"

He smiled again. "Yes, it does, little man." Eli half-smiled at the term. John put on a tough face. "But don't you worry. It won't hurt for much longer." He squeezed Eli's small hand. "Be strong, little guy. Take care of Caroline and Anne if... if something happens, okay?"

Eli nodded. His chest puffed out with pride at the responsibility.

"Anne, why are you hiding back there?" John teased. His lightness twisted my heartstrings. *Cheerful as always, even when he's...* I couldn't even think it.

"Because I don't like it when you yell," she whimpered from behind Rachel's skirt.

He chuckled. "I won't yell again if I can help it," he said, extending a hand to her. She crept closer.

He reached out for a hug. Anne fell on John's torso. He grimaced with pain and shivered, then threw an arm over her small body.

She sat up, sitting astride of him. "I love you this much, John," she declared, holding her hands out as far as they could go.

A tear made its way out of his eye in perfect synchrony with the drop of water coming out of mine.

"I love you more," he teased.

"Nu-uh, I love YOU more!"

She grinned at the same time he did. He lifted a weak hand and tickled her belly. She giggled and John hugged her one last time. I picked her off of him — I doubted she understood what was happening, even after seeing Mama and Papa die. The thought made me cry even harder, if possible.

"Caroline, there are some things I want you to know," he said. "Mama told me first because you were upset with moving and she didn't want to upset you more. She intended to tell you someday, but I guess she didn't get around to it.

"Great-Grandmother Pamela has an illness. There is a cure, but it can't be found in her state. In fact, it's only found in Illinois. You must get to her with the cure, or she will not survive." He paused.

"But what *is* the cure? And why won't someone just get it for her?"

"The cure is the bulb of a plant called the Hydra. Be careful; it only blooms in October, so since this is July, you'll have to hurry. You'll find out when you get there why they don't import it for her." He screwed up his face and took a series of shallow breaths. "I don't think... I have long." He grabbed my shoulders, "Caroline, they're depending on you," John said.

He convulsed and his eyes rolled back. My heart leapt into my throat. This was happening. I heard a scream coming from myself. With these words, he writhed on the ground, eyes rolled back into his head.

He lay still.

Not My Fault

WITHIN THOSE FOUR days my life flipped upside down.

Instead of the original six members of my family, we now had three. With close to no plan, no food, and no money, our situation seemed hopeless. At least Rachel had let us stay with her until we could get back on our feet. I sighed and looked out the window with my chin in my hands, much as I had done every day for the past two weeks and three days. My thoughts veered back to our situation. *We have* nothing! I felt bitter. *I don't know how to do this!* My thoughts took the opportunity to prod me in my weak spot. *It* was *all my fault he died. If only I hadn't gotten involved with his brother, he wouldn't have been angry, and John wouldn't have had to fight for me, and he wouldn't have gotten hurt, and*—I sniffed and sat up straighter as I took a deep breath to collect myself. There was no use in crying. I needed to pull myself together. As John had said, they were depending on me to take charge. *It's time to move on.* "And I mean it this time," I said out loud. I gritted my teeth and stood.

I put on the clean green dress Rachel had given me, washed the tears from my face, and collected my hair in a neat little knot at the back of my neck. I turned to the mirror and assessed my appearance. *Well,* I reflected bitterly. *At least I look less the beggar than I did before we got here.* I straightened my care-worn shoulders, took in a deep breath, and opened the pine door of the bedroom. As I passed it was difficult to avoid glancing at the chair where John had fallen. That chair alone grew dusty; all the others had been sat in but none of us could bring ourselves to be seated in that one. I strode to Eli, Anne, and Rachel, where they sat dejected with a freshly-baked batch of cookies. None of the three of them spoke. Rachel, cheery spirit she was, kept opening her mouth to say something, her eyes brightening. Then she saw our faces and slumped back down in her chair.

With a half-smile I sat beside them. "Eli — Anne — I think it's time we were on our way."

They both nodded slowly. Rachel pursed her lips and looked off into the sidelines.

"Whatever you think," she said, a hint of disappointment in her smooth voice.

I was glad she was so unemotional about it — I had been worried she would be able to convince me to stay if she tried.

As the afternoon waned on, we said our tender and tearful goodbyes to Rachel and started on our way. I held the bucket of cookies which Rachel insisted we take. Once again we made our way through the woods. We soon arrived at the place where we had decided to bury John. On Rachel's land and in fact using stone quarried from her property for the headstone, we had given John a decent resting place. His headstone read,

Here lies John,

Beloved one,

Now but not forever gone.

Born July 1842

Died July 31 1856

I crouched down to the silent headstone, wishing he was still there with me. I let my fingers brush the cold rock. I drew in a ragged breath, picked up a crumble of dirt, and crushed it between my fingers. "Goodbye, John," I whispered.

Anne and Eli stood a respectful distance away, letting me say my final goodbyes by myself. We all knew, we would never see his grave again. As I stood and joined my remaining two siblings, Eli's turn came. With a slow pace he walked to the sad spot, his hands shoved deep into his pockets.

I refused to watch. I endured the pain of staring at his grave once. I placed my back to John's grave, holding a protective hand on the squirmy Anne.

The forest itself seemed to share our sorrow. The trees blew back and forth, their leafy branches rushing a whispery goodbye. The tumbling stream felt like the forest's tears pouring out in a long river. The animals stopping to stare at us for a moment were halting to pay their respects. A breeze blew by, trying to get one last glimpse of the beloved boy whom they had blown over so often. The clouds shaded us from the sun.

I pushed the three of us ahead as hard as we could go; if you're tired you don't have enough energy for grief. I would not lose another sibling. Whatever it took, I would not lose another one.

I grimaced as the thought I tried to avoid rushed into my mind. *Who was I kidding- I know it was my fault! There's no getting around it. I should've seen it coming!* My hands curled into a tight fist, piercing little crescents in my palm. Eli put a hand on my arm gently. He patted it and then moved on. I didn't turn to see him, glad to skip the pitying look. I took a deep breath and tried to dwell on how John said it wasn't my fault. I unclenched and reclenched my hands, reacting to the flood of emotions raging through me. Once again I was plagued by my own thoughts. *Caroline, you* know *it was your fault. You should've saved him.* "No," I muttered, "I couldn't have done anything." *Yes, you could've! Why didn't you give up the necklace sooner? He could've been saved if you had...* "I don't know that," I said with indignation. My ears were getting warm with raised circulation. *Oh, but I think you do.* "No, I don't!" *You can tell yourself it wasn't your fault, but the easiest person to lie to is yourself.* "It WASN'T my FAULT!" I yelled. Eli and Anne jumped and turned around.

"Caroline!" Eli asked. "Are you alright?"

I stopped walking. My cooped-up thoughts came rushing out as the floodgates of tears opened. "No! It was my fault John died. I could've — should've — done something. I'm the one who distracted him and gave the sheriff a chance to hurt him. It's all my fault." I put my hands on my face as I sat in the dusty path.

"Caroline, you know it wasn't your fault! There's nothing you could've done about it," Eli comforted.

"I know nothing of the sort. I don't know. I just…" I tried to wipe away some tears. They kept coming. "I feel so unworthy. I can't do this. I've already lost John and Mama and Papa… I just can't help but wonder—" My voice grew quiet and I stared at the ground. "What's to stop me from losing you two?"

Eli lifted my hands off of my teary red face, staring deep into my eyes. "You can lead us, Caroline. I have faith in you." He held my hands, cleared his throat, and put on a 'reciting voice.' "Deuteronomy 31:6 — 'Be strong and courageous. Do not be afraid or terrified because of them, for the LORD your God goes with you; He will never leave you nor forsake you.'" He had a brave smile. It shone through the layer of grime and sweat and tears on his face like the most beautiful lamp in the world.

I smiled gently.

He grinned and gave me a reassuring hug. "Come on, let's go," he coaxed.

I got up and my knees popped. We trudged forward.

I felt the hand of peace come on me as we walked in silence. After all, I had asked John how he felt. I don't think even he knew there was a problem until the end, so how could I be expected to know? And besides, he told me not to think it was my fault.

My stomach grumbled and it reminded me of John's ability to get food for us. He was always ready to hunt whenever we were hungry. Just like the time he woke up early and brought the rabbits to thank me. I smiled through the tears. Was that only three weeks ago? Memories of him flooded my mind. When he took Anne in his arms, volunteering to give up his chance to speak with Papa for the last time. Instead he watched me talk to our dying parent. When I ran to find the sheriff and he stayed with the others, and of how he tried to talk me out of going to the fair in the first place. My last memory of John fighting for me made my heart melt.

I decided I owed it to John to get the other two to Great-Grandmother Pamela's. And maybe by saving Great-Grandmother Pamela my spirit would get some closure; I would feel like John's mission was completed.

I licked my lips. *Now I am the closest thing to an adult for the children. They need me... I'm not responsible for John's death.* I repeated the chant in my head. *They need me... I didn't cause his death.* I felt strength and clarity repeating the difficult words. *They need me, and John's death was not my fault.* The beat of the words set the rhythm for my feet hitting the ground. I glanced at my siblings and realized Anne was trailing far behind me, her dolly dragging on the ground and tears wetting her dirty face.

I walked to her and crouched down to her level. She looked up at me with hope. I managed a weak smile and held out my arms. I knew first-hand the grief she felt. She rushed into my arms and squeezed me.

"I'm sad, Boo," she murmured.

This time I didn't even hear the nickname. "Me too."

Eli joined our group. I no longer felt the drive of the chant. We sat together, hugging each other in the understanding of our loss.

After several minutes we dried our eyes and stood, the sound of some sniffles breaking the silence. We held hands as we walked down the path and didn't look back.

We Make Friends with an Enemy

IN SEVENTEEN DAYS we found ourselves near the Missouri border.

"Say, Caroline," Eli started. A smile pulled at the upper corner of his sweaty lips. I glanced at him and raised my eyebrows. "Remember the time John went to town for the first time?"

I chuckled, nodded, and wiped the salty sweat from my brow.

Anne cocked her head. "What are you talking about?" she inquired.

"You don't remember that?" he asked incredulously. "Oh yes, of course. You weren't born yet. Well, it went like this.

"John begged Mama and Papa to let him go with Papa to town. That's when Papa did what he called 'man's business': doing the shopping and trading in town and getting the news. After weeks of begging, they said he could go. He wouldn't stop talking about it!" Eli turned to me. "Remember that?" I smiled and nodded. We walked a little faster without realizing it. "Then, when the next Saturday came, John woke up hours earlier than he had to. He was so excited, he awoke Papa, too. A very excited John and a very sleepy Papa came into town before people were up and about. When they arrived, Papa went on an errand which allowed John some free time to strut his new "manhood." So he was walking around outside, waiting until the general store opened before he could make his orders. From right behind him, the Widow Talan strutted out of her beautiful new door and seated herself in her carriage, holding a fancy white parasol and wearing a new red velvet dress." He made silly faces and began walking around in a condescending mimicry of the rich woman. Anne started laughing. I glanced over at them and chuckled. "Oddly enough, however, there was no stable-boy following her. And John ducked behind a sack of flour, because," he looked around in mock suspicion and whispered behind his hand, "she was rumored to keep little children in her basement as slaves!" He wiggled his eyebrows profusely.

Anne gasped with horror. "No!" she cried. She made a gesture of disbelief.

"Oh, but yes!" he asserted. I giggled and gave Eli a gentle slap on the back. "Elijah Eric! Don't tell such tales!"

He shrugged in child-like innocence. "Alright, so I stretched it a little bit." He grinned.

"So," he continued, "Wait — where was I?"

Anne covered her mouth and flashed her eyes from side to side, looking around nervously. "The part about the horrible old witch who kept cute little girls as slaves!!" I smiled at her additions.

"Oh! Yes. So, he was hiding behind a sack of flour, but little did he know the top of his head was visible, which meant the hawk-eyed Widow noticed him. She shouted in that nasal voice of hers, 'Hello there, you! Boy!'" Eli imitated an over-exaggerated version of a woman's high-pitched voice. "'Me?' he asked in an innocent sounding tone." Eli drew out the word and pointed to himself, as John would have. I laughed as Eli started to enjoy his narration more and more. "'Well, of course you! Who else would I be talking to — myself? I'm not that far gone, sonny!' said the Widow. So John stood and stared at her. 'Well? What are you waiting for? Come over here!' she cried. So John walked over there, *fainting* with fear!" He slapped his hand to his forehead and fell to the ground dramatically. I snorted at his acting. He sat up on his elbow. "When he was near enough to touch, she grabbed him by the shirt collar and began speaking to him." He had stood up as he demonstrated the shirt-grabbing part of his story. "'Now lookee here, boy. My stable-boy snuck off to care for his sick mother, so I have no one to saddle my horses up for me! If you'll do it for me, I'll pay you a gold dollar!' And she held up a shiny, brand-new gold dollar, big as the sun."

Now he and Anne stood shoulder to shoulder, pretending to see the gold dollar. He ran his hand over the horizon. Anne was most entranced.

"Golly… it's so pretty," she sighed. She reached out as if to touch the imaginary coin.

Eli pulled her hand back, staring at her in shock. "Watch it!" he cried. "That's John's, remember?"

She withdrew her hand in repentance. He continued.

"Now he figured he was a man now, and a man needs to earn some income. So he decided to do it. By this time, the sun was up and several people had begun gathering in the streets, opening their shops. John ran into the Widow's stables, picked out the two nearest horses, and led them by the reins to where her carriage was sitting. He had never hooked up a horse and carriage by himself before, since he was only nine, but he was doing the best he could. In the meantime, the Widow Talan stood by her carriage, all in a huff. He finished hooking everything up, and told her he was done. So she gave him the gold dollar and climbed in. 'Giddyap!' she yelled. The horses took off running." He once again leaned down to Anne's level. "But guess what?"

"What?" she whispered.

"The carriage didn't!" His voice rose as he straightened up. "John had forgotten to tie the knot in the harness, so when the horses took off running, the leather pulled out of the metal ring! So the high part, where she was sitting, fell down onto the ground, taking her with it. She was stunned — just sitting there on the ground, not moving or saying a word, and her hair was all messed up, and her fancy hat was all crooked over one eye…" here Eli trailed off with laughter. "And — and her brand-new dress was all splayed out over the dirt —" He rocked with laughter. "And — and then! And then, a wind came and blew off her hat and *her hair came with it!* She had been wearing a wig the whole time, and no one even knew! So..." He didn't have enough breath to keep going. After a moment he continued, his laughter tapering off. "So everyone was awake now and they were all laughing, and she just started yelling at John, and he was trying to apologize and having to shout it over all the chaos..." He and Anne started laughing again. They were both rolling around on the ground, laughing so hard they were crying. I also was laughing, though I was leaning against a tree and not lying on the ground.

After several moments our laughter tapered off again. I was wiping my eyes and kept breaking out into sporadic laughter as Eli finished his story. "So anyway, just then Papa walked out, and seeing everyone laughing at her and John apologizing, he just took him by the hand, muttered an apology to the Widow, helped her stand up, seated John on our horse, and rode home without another word but his laughter!"

He grinned.

I resolved to make it through the day without any major problems or distractions. After all, it was the beginning of September. That meant I had two months in which to cross Missouri and get to Illinois in time for the flower to bloom.

Then only one more month to finish the rest of our journey before winter. The odds were not in our favor that we would survive an unaided trip in the harsh, biting winter. I quickened my pace.

We walked in silence about ten minutes. Eli's stomach roared.

"Sorry!" He grinned.

"I'm getting hungry too. What about you, Anne?"

She nodded, clinging to my sweaty arm. "Me too."

"Alright then, let's stop for a food break. Eli, why don't you and Anne go right over there and look for some berries, and I'll go on the other side to look for something to eat."

They skipped to the right side of the road, behind the thick foliage. I ducked under branches on the left side. "Don't eat anything unless you're positive it's not poisonous!" I warned.

Two muffled voices came from the other side. "We won't!" "Yeah!"

I chuckled at their childish eagerness. I found a raspberry bush and prepared to call for their aid in picking the berries.

Suddenly, from within the forest, I thought I heard someone yell. I paused, but found myself listening to silence. I resumed harvesting the berries.

But this time the call was definite.

"Help! Please, someone help me!"

"Eli! Anne! Come here, quickly!" I shouted calling them to me.

They crashed through the bushes before I had even finished speaking. I stared at Eli with a raised eyebrow, wondering how they both heard me and came so quickly.

"We heard it, too," he explained.

We followed the calls. But the deeper we went into the forest, the more lost we got. Soon it seemed like the voice came from all directions, and as soon as we'd turn and go the way it sounded, it seemed to come from the opposite direction.

"We're coming, but we can't find you! Just keep shouting and we'll get there as soon as we can," I yelled.

There was a pause. Then it resumed.

"You can't find me?".

"Not yet, but I will!"

Who was the voice? It was on the tip of my tongue, but then I heard another shout.

"Okay, I'll keep shouting!" the voice answered.

After thirty minutes of fruitless effort to find the person in need, we stumbled upon a rotting old cabin. The molding door hung open, its hinges rusting fit to fall off. The one window consisted of sharp slivers of glass planted in the frame. Oddly contrasting with the disarray of the outside, however, a cheery light shone from within. We ran inside, expecting to find the boy who was shouting. The firelight and a multitude of filled bottles greeted us. I circled the well-provisioned room, confused.

"I'm out here!" he shouted.

We headed outside. What
we found was most
interesting: next to a pile of
chopped wood stood a
bare-footed, dirty boy
holding an axe.

I didn't stop to see his
face but first noticed he was
not 'holding' the axe in
either of his *hands*.

The axe lay embedded in
the grimy, overweight boy's foot. The more pressing
problem, however, was there was a heavy wheel on his foot.
I nodded in understanding—it appeared to be the reason he
dropped the axe in the first place and also why he didn't get
it out yet. He couldn't move out from under the wheel.

I had never had a strong stomach for disgusting things.
However, I knew what needed to be done. I braced myself
and crouched down, preparing to yank out the axe.

I gasped and looked up. "World of wonders!" I cried. Eli
told me later my face drained of all color. "Henry
Williams?" I asked incredulously.

The axe had cloven the tell-tale birthmark in two.

He smiled bitterly, his eyes betraying his agony. "Hello,
Caroline." He gasped, shuddering. He reached out to me.
"Caroline — please help me!"

I slunk backwards, shocked to find him here. And
needing my help. Of all people. All the terrible deeds he did
flashed through my mind. The time he pushed me in the
mud. When he tried to drown my kitten. The time I saw

him steal our chicken and then blame me for it. When he threw my best doll in the pond. When he made a laughing-stock of me at school on my first day.

He had made my life miserable. My first impulse was to turn my back on him and leave. I studied his face, attempting to see whether or not he was thinking about what he had done to me as well. In his eyes I read pain. He looked somehow older than I remembered, more experienced in responsibilities. This new, mature look surprised me. I didn't know he was capable of it.

"Please," he reiterated.

I looked back at Eli and Anne. They were both watching to see what I would do. I wasn't going to let Henry be more mature than me, nor was I going to show Eli and Anne a bad example of holding a grudge. I took a deep breath and stepped closer to Henry, making my hand meet his. I squeezed it and gazed into his grungy blue eyes.

"Jesus says to love our enemies and pray for those who persecute us. I'll help you."

Gratitude and relief replaced the pain in his eyes. I braced myself then kneeled down in the bloody dirt. Looking away, I wrapped my hands around the cold metal handle and yanked. Hard. A disgusting sound ensued, like your foot when you pull it out of mud or like when you pull a weed out of the river. It was more a sucking sound than anything else.

I came near to vomiting after this ordeal, but Henry seemed unconcerned. As soon as the instrument was discharged from him, he grasped his profusely-bleeding foot and hopped inside. The sight was almost funny; only my shock and tumultuous stomach prevented laughter. I followed, knowing very well it would need to be bandaged or else it could get infected.

I recalled when Papa suffered a bite on the arm by the neighbor's horse. Mama took a pot and instructed me to fill it with water, which I did. Lugging the pot full of water, I stumbled back inside. She told me to boil it, so I went back outside and put it on the hot outdoor stove. While I waited for it to boil, I stood half-hiding behind the chimney, watching Papa groan. When the water bubbled up, Mama took the cleanest cloth we had, dropped it into the steaming liquid, let it billow inside the pot for a moment, and then plucked it out with her hands. I remember being amazed at what marvelous control she had over her nerves. She touched such hot water without shrinking back. I later learned her adrenaline and concern for Papa had allowed for such control. She calmly wrung out the cloth then marched over to Papa. Lifting up his bloody arm, she applied the bandage. He howled with pain. She ignored his cries as she tied the cloth around his arm and applied pressure to stop the bleeding.

I intended to do the same. Building up my confidence, I nodded and reached to swing the door open.

I froze, trying to remember what Mama had done next. Was it to tell him to rest? Did she open the window, giving him fresh air? Did she feed him berries to thicken the blood? What *was* it?

I shrugged. Ah, well. I said a quick prayer I would remember when it came time to copy her actions.

My stomach didn't like the idea of what I had to do. I rubbed it and proceeded to open the cabin door.

As I walked in, Henry eased onto the only furniture in the house, a ripped-up chair. His foot sat below him on the dirt floor. He stared at me with expectation, his arms folded across his chest.

I cleared my throat. There was no backup plan to this; no adult to help me if I messed up; no other plan but me. If I did even one little thing wrong, Henry could die. My stomach rolled over again.

I whispered a little prayer and went with my instinct.

"Eli, start a fire outside." He rushed off to do the job. "Henry, where's a kettle?" He pointed to a cabinet under a shelf filled with bottles of berries. Anne reached under there and brought out Henry's tea-kettle. The sides and top were so brown with rust I could not see any silver. The rusty handle fell off when Anne touched it. I hesitated at the rustiness, but then recovered my vigor, remembering it was all we had. "Fill it up with water at the creek just down the road," I commanded. She rushed off. "Henry, lie down on the ground and put your foot up on the chair." He started to do as I commanded but was wincing at the pain and moving too slowly. I knelt and helped him prop it up.

Though I told him to prop up his foot, I don't know why I did; it just seemed like the best thing for him to do. Hence my belief in God's intervention.

I examined his foot. It bled profusely, but it was clean blood — no clumps in it. I recalled that's what Doctor Lambdin had described as a sign of a clean cut. I stood and rifled through the cabinets and up on shelves for a clean cloth. *Or a cloth of any sort, for that matter.*

"Caroline, what are you looking for?" Henry asked.

"Hold on a moment," I said.

I still found no fabric.

"Henry, do you have any cloths?" I asked.

He shook his head. "I could've told you minutes ago this is all I've got," he said, indicating his clothes.

I sucked in, trying to figure a way to bandage his foot with nothing to use for bandages. I blushed as a thought came to me, but then forced the flush away. I found I only had one option. I turned my back to Henry and, still colored a tomato red, tore a section off my petticoat. Henry was staring at the ceiling, being a gentleman for once and pretending not to notice what I had done.

"Alright, bring your foot over here," I asked.

He obliged. I measured the cloth around his foot — the length was perfect for two or three wrappings.

Eli walked into the cabin. "Caroline," he stated, "the fire's hot and ready."

"Alright, now go put the —"

"Anne already put the water on to boil several minutes ago."

I smiled at how easy my siblings predicted me. "Alright, thanks. I can't do anything until then, so please tell me when it's ready." I watched him nod and walk out of the room.

I was startled to look up and find Henry watching me. I, in turn, stared at him. "Caroline," he started gently.

"Yes?" I replied. I stood and tried to look busy, though I longed to know for what topic he might use that tone.

"I want to thank you for helping me. I... I know I take a lot of getting used to." He eyed his hands and fidgeted.

I chuckled and nodded. "Yes, you do."

"Do you think —" he started. He stopped and glanced the other direction.

I turned to him and stopped trying to look busy. "What did you say?"

"Nothing. Never mind. Don't worry about it."

"No, really. Tell me!"

"I can't. Never mind! Forget I said anything." He waved a hand in the air.

"Henry Williams, I will walk away and let you fix this foot yourself!" I threatened, hoping he couldn't hear the pounding in my ears.

He smiled in return. "Well... I wanted to know if you could find it in your heart to forgive me. I realize how unreasonable that must sound to you after all of the horrible things I've done to you. I just feel so bad ..." He chuckled bitterly. "I know, it's a ridiculous request, right? Why would you ever forgive me?"

He looked down, ashamed. I walked to him and took his hand. He glanced up into my eyes, surprised. I smiled.

"The Bible says in Colossians 3:13, 'Bear with each other and forgive one another if any of you has a grievance against someone. Forgive as the Lord forgave you.' So... I forgive you." I smiled. An impish grin grew across my face as I added, "But please — don't be the same Henry I knew."

A wide grin spread across his face. "Thank you," he declared. After a moment, he added, "And I don't think I will be the same, either."

Eli walked into the room. "The waters about ready," he declared.

"Alright, I'll be right there."

I stood and walked to the boiling pot of water. I dropped the more-or-less clean cloth into the steamy pot and prepared to pick it up. My reserve to reach into the pot diminished with each second I stood and stared into the bubbling, steaming water.

A bright idea occurred to me. I took the hot water and poured it out, but saved the soaked cloth; that way I wouldn't have to touch the water. Holding the nevertheless searing hot cloth by the corner, I toted the makeshift bandage inside. Henry waited on the ground.

"Alright, here we go." I knelt down to his foot and he looked away. "Now hold still. This might sting a little." I proceeded to pull the cloth nearer his foot.

"Wait!" he interrupted.

"Oh, don't be such a cry-baby. You'll be fine," I assured.

"No, it's not that. I just wanted you to please get me the jar of Sugar-flower leaves."

"I will, right after I bandage you." I brought the rapidly-cooling bandage nearer.

"No, wait! I need it now!"

"Why?" I protested.

"Just trust me, I'll explain in a minute."

I sighed and stood. "Fine. Which one is it?" There were so many jars it was difficult to distinguish which was which.

"The one to the left of that one … no, farther … farther … two shelves down … yes, that's it!"

I selected said jar and handed it to him. "Are you quite finished wasting this bandage now?"

To my surprise he opened the lid, pulled out an eight-inch leaf, and put it in his mouth. With a full mouth, he replied, "Actually, it wasn't a waste of time — this is a rare plant that prevents pain."

I was too busy wrapping, taking off, and re-wrapping the cloth to notice what he had said, but as I began to get the hang of wrapping, I had time to think about it.

"Henry, how did you know about that plant? And what are all these jars in here?"

He shrugged. "They're all plants I collected for different uses, and I traded someone in town for the jars. I just know plants, having spent most of my time in the forest. It's useful to know these things when you're alone. For instance, this stuff," he took a jar off of the ground next to him and opened the lid, "is called Juji juice. It's useful for writing with. The only drawback is the smell, its' really, really bad." He smiled and put the jar back. "This one is interesting and very rare but useful — it's the anti-venom for many animal bites. You can always tell it's the right plant because of the rare pink color. Or here's a very special one," he bragged. "This one makes some animals, like rabbits or frogs or squirrels, come to eat it. But when they come and take a bite, something in there paralyzes them for twenty minutes. So anyone who knows what the plant is can use it to catch some dinner." He rubbed his stomach as it growled. "Speaking of which, what are we having?"

I rolled my eyes and chuckled.

We sipped some delicious soup made of Henry's berries and plant roots. "So, Henry, why are you here?" I asked.

"It's kind of a long story. I'm sure you don't want to hear it." He studied his bowl of soup.

"Well, it's not like I have anything else to do right now."

He conceded, shrugging. "The day before your house burned down, Garret Powerly came over — remember him?" I nodded with grim recollection. "He was not what you would call an honest gentleman," he whispered to Eli and Anne, leaning over in their direction. "Well, we decided to sneak down to the cellar and have some of Ma's prize apples. Then he got an idea. I tried to stop him, but…" he shook his head.

"Anyway. Madison Jenkins accused him of pushing her on the playground that morning, and she found some 'witnesses' to support her story. The teacher paddled him in front of the whole school, and he was real steamed about it.

"So his idea was to take Ma's onions, which she had been cultivating for months. Then wait until the night-time, and throw 'em in Maddies Pa's well. That would make the water taste and smell like nasty onions. That takes a lot of money to fix and he knew it.

I tried to convince him not to do it, but he was stubborn as ever.

'Why, Henry Williams, are you sayin' you're not gonna do what I told ya to?' he said.

'Well, no, Garret, but I don't think —'

'What you think don't matter. I'm older, and I'm in charge, and you just better do it!' he yelled as he took me by the shirt collar.

I slapped his hand. 'You know I don't like to be handled like that, Garret.' I brushed my shirt off.

He smirked. 'Handle this, Henry.' He stuffed about ten good-sized onions in my shirt. 'And don't even think 'bout taking 'em out, neither.' He sneered again and warned me with a readied fist. As a second thought, he added in a mocking tone, 'And don't even think about blabbering to yer mommy!' His voice grew deeper. 'If you do…' He made a fist again and stood in a fighting stance. I took a deep breath and nodded.

"So he forced me to hide some of her onions in my shirt, and he did the same, and we snuck out the door. Then we walked over to the Jenkins place and began to chuck all those onions in the water. Well, we were checking over our shoulder pretty constantly, but we didn't do it well enough, 'cause soon we heard a voice speak. Near scared me right out of my socks.

"Whaddya think you're doin'?" Old Man Jenkins asked, a whisper of anger in his voice.

"I stared straight into the barrel of his rifle. I dropped the onions and threw my hands up in the air. He continued,

'I said, what're you kids doing on my property! And don't give me any lies, neither, because I've been standing here the whole time. Now come on, confess.'

"I was too dumbfounded for words, but sure enough Garret wasn't. 'It was all his idea, Mr. Jenkins, sir! He forced me to come with him and said he'd beat me up if I didn't!'

"I gave him a wide-eyed stare.

"Jenkins looked us both up and down. 'Are you trying to tell me a large, able boy like yourself feels threatened by this little squirt?'

"Of course I felt the need to protest, so I did. But that's not the point. Long story short, Garret somehow convinced Old Man Jenkins it was all my idea and he was innocent. So he let Garret go but led me back to my house — at gunpoint! He stood outside the house and started yelling at the top of his lungs for Ma to come outside, which she did, in a hurry. The lateness of the hour and the nightgown she wore — which was not nearly decent enough for company — made her extra mad. As soon as she was outside, he began yelling at Ma to keep me under a watchful eye before I did any more damage, or else he would have the sheriff after me, he said.

"Pretty soon he stormed off. I tried to scurry before Ma caught me, but she grabbed me before I could get away and gave me a sound licking. After that, she sat me down and told me if I didn't change my behavior then she would wash her hands of me, and she would fetch the sheriff herself if she had to. So of course I promised to stop, and she sent me to bed without supper or promise of breakfast.

"Then, later that night, I woke up to hear this strange noise below me. Almost, like whispering. I drifted back to sleep, thinking I was dreaming, but then I remembered the mule-headedness of that Garret. Sure 'nough, when I went down to see what was going on in our root cellar, there was Garret and his gang, all filled up with onions and getting ready to go dump 'em in the Jenkins' pond again! I tried to stop 'em, but they wouldn't listen. But by this time, I guess Ma had heard the boys, too, because just then she stormed down there with a lit candle, and saw all of us down there just chock-full of her onions. She commenced to screaming something horrible, and told us all to 'jest git off'n her prop'rty,' or else she'd go call the sheriff on 'em, she said. After she had said that, she got bent over and started coughing something horrid — the kind of coughing that comes from deep down and keeps rolling out; y'know?" We all nodded at the unpleasant recollection of such pain. After a moment, I leaned over and put a hand on his shoulder. He looked up and continued, licking his lips and wiping his nose on his sleeve. He threw a quick glance around the room to gauge our expressions. "So, um, we all had to go away, and then when she saw I was one of the boys in the lot, she took me by the shirt collar, deposited me outside without a word, and locked the door. So I walked, and I guess that's how I got here." He shrugged as he finished his narrative. He wiped his running nose with the back of his hand again.

"World of wonders," I said. I shook my head. My parents had been nothing like that, thank goodness.

I gazed at him for a moment, a question forming in my mind. "Henry, how—" I stopped myself and waved my hand in the air in a dismissive gesture.

"What?"

"Never mind, sorry." My cheeks burned.

"If you're wondering how I got to be so good at grammar and whatnot since I never went to school... Well, I may be good at speaking, but I'm not good at much else," he confessed with a halfhearted smile.

I blushed and turned my head, embarrassed he should read my gaze so well. Eli asked, "So! Where is 'here?'"

"Just two or so miles that way," he pointed to east, "is Lexington in Lafayette County."

"Lafayette County?" asked Eli incredulously.

"Yeessss...." Henry replied.

"As in *the* Lafayette County?"

"At least, I think so," he replied.

Eli slapped his forehead. "I never thought... Who'd have thought — *the* Lafayette County! Good night! How did I not realize?" He walked half away from the circle, muttering to himself. "Well?" I cried. "What is it?"

He turned to me, astonished. "Caroline, we're not coming up on the border of Missouri..." he said. "We're in the middle! We already passed the edge!"

"*What?*"

"Yep, we're about halfway in. There's about — oh," Henry started.

"270 miles until Springfield, Illinois, then 340 miles to Springfield, Ohio," Eli finished, again using his fascination and studies with mileage.

"How did we get this far without noticing?"

"'Only 610 miles until Great's," Anne interjected.

We all turned and stared at her. "She's right," Eli added, sounding impressed.

We all stared at her, astounded. "Anne, that adding was amazing!" I exclaimed. "You're learning quick," I said, patting her back.

"Well," Eli blustered, puffing out his chest, "she's learning from the best." He dusted off his shoulders jokingly.

I laughed. "Wait a minute… Anne, why did you call her 'Great'?" I asked. "Because 'Great… Great-Grandmother Pam'la' is too hard to say," she said, her eyes wide and vulnerable. She gave a dimpled smile and cocked her head, her blond curls falling around her face.

I felt the sudden urge to give her a hug. I set her on my lap and gave in to the rare whim.

Henry said, "We'll talk more in the morning. For now, let's all go sleep."

We settled down and slept. It was a relief. Unfortunately, it was also one of the last peaceful rests I would experience for a long time.

Things Get Serious

NINE DAYS AND an unbelievable 110 miles later familiar sounds of laughter reached my ears. This would be our last day together. Henry decided to set off on a different direction.

Thinking about these I wandered over to a tree trunk and leaned against the fragrant but moldy wood. Anne sat perched on top of Henry's shoulders, holding his unruly, light brown hair like the reigns of a horse. His long, pale ears poked out of the curls in his hair. Henry stood and wobbled with false unsteady footing as he tickled Eli below him. Anne bounced and clutched his hair in her little hands, giggling. Henry was smiling and chuckling, holding Eli upside-down and now right-side up, now splayed on the ground and then up in the air. All three were flushed with happy exertion, grinning and making the forest echo with laughter. Henry happened to glance over in my direction in a momentary lapse of concentration. He sent a roguish grin in my direction. I smiled.

"Alright, guys, time for a break," he laughed, exhausted but happy.

"Thank you, Henry," I offered.

"For what?" He leaned on the tree next to me.

"For putting a smile back on their faces," I said, looking him in the face. "It means a lot to me. It's not easy to do that anymore. You know —" I hesitated and cut myself off, picking up a stick and walking towards the ashes of last night's fire.

"What?" he prompted as he followed me.

I stirred the ashes, making them smolder. "Well, I guess I was just going to say the way you were playing with them reminded me of John."

"Oh. I see..." he trailed off. He clapped his hands together and spoke. "Well! Let's get some good breakfast going before you leave." He rubbed his hands and started to walk away.

"Um, actually, Henry, I've been meaning to talk to you about that... well, I mean... I know you'd already decided to go west, but I was wondering if you'd like to stay with us for the rest of the way. I mean, after all, my siblings and I sure wouldn't mind another person to keep us company, and I'm sure you need help just as much as we do, and besides —" Deciding to put a lighter note on the subject, I added, "And besides, someone needs to keep an eye on you." I glanced at him from the corner of my eye and grinned slowly, gauging his reaction.

He heaved a sigh. "Sounds great," he said. He quickened the pace of his words as he finished his sentence. "But… if we're going on a journey, we need food! So I'd better get some." I narrowed my eyes at him. I wondered what he was going to say before he changed his mind? He continued, avoiding my stare. "So! Listen up, you may need this. Having spent lots of time in the forest, I learned it is possible to hunt squirrels by sitting up in the branches and waiting for them to come to you. So I'm going to go get some meat, alright?"

"That would be wonderful," I said, still suspicious.

He stood and left.

Three hours later, he returned with some freshly-killed squirrels. I skinned them, dropping them into the pot so as not to burn myself. For the ninth day with Henry with us, we ate a hearty meal. Gobbling down the delicious, juicy, hot meat, I observed my new friend and siblings, and I smiled. Henry was laughing as Eli told a joke and Anne was sitting on his lap, happy and unconcerned. Though the past few months had been hard, God blessed us with all we needed and some of what we wanted; it was more than enough for me.

"Anne," I said, "eat your food. You can talk to Henry all you want later, but right now is the time for eating."

Her face fell. "I don't like it," she whined.

"I don't care. You need that food to walk and to function. Eat it."

"Nooo…" she whined, climbing down from Henry's lap and flopping down on the ground. "It's too hot."

I sighed and helped her blow it off. "Now eat it," I said.

"Don't wanna…" she whined again.

"Well, why not?" I demanded.

She struggled for a moment, searching for a reason she thought I'd accept. "It's too… cold."

"No, it's not."

"Yes, it is. And it's icky."

I lost my patience. "Dorothy Anne! Just eat your food!" I shouted.

There was silence as I shoveled the food into my mouth and the boys picked at their meals, afraid to look up, joke, or bother me lest they be my next victims. "Everyone else, too!" I demanded.

Afraid to disobey, they took their forks and devoured the food.

Except Anne did not.

"Anne…" I threatened. She sensed the fire in my eyes and made up yet another excuse. "I need some water first!"

"Fine," I snapped. "Why don't you go get some, then?" I turned my back to her, knowing well she would never venture off alone.

With a pitiful look of fear, she stuck out her bottom lip and made it quiver. I rolled my eyes. It wasn't going to work; I myself had taught her that trick. "But… but Boo, I want you to come with me," she whimpered.

"I can't. I am eating."

She huffed and wandered behind me.

I kept an eye on her over my shoulder.

About twenty feet out, she stopped and climbed down into a hole small enough I could still see her head. "Boo, it's dirty water," she shouted.

"Well, I can't see it," my tone grew pointed, "since I'm EATING." I sighed. "I'm sure it's fine. Don't worry about it."

"I don't want this water," she whined.

"Look, either drink it or don't. I don't care. Just do it and get back here!" I watched her slurp up three handfuls of water.

"Done," she announced.

"Come on back, then," I said.

She did. Having run out of excuses, she ate her food.

Soon we had all finished our plates of food. With full bellies, we picked up the jars we had brought with us of Henry's most precious berries and were on our way.

Again I pushed our pace onward until late that night. By my calculations, we made an impressive twenty-two miles that day. The sounds of talking died as we dropped into a deep and exhausted sleep.

Anne and Eli lay sprawled on the ground, Anne's hair splayed out in every direction. I sighed as I crouched and smoothed it down. I placed her dolly in her arm. She snuffled and rolled over on her side. I gave into my emotions and leaned down to her face, planting a small kiss on her fat, babyish cheek. I stroked her hair as I thought over the past several months. "I… I love you, Anne," I whispered. Although she was half-asleep, this heartfelt confession somehow made its way into her brain.

"Mmm…" she mumbled. She reached up in a 'pick me up' gesture.

"Oh," I whispered. I picked her up, trying not to drop her or wake her up, and cradled her lovingly against my shoulder. I lowered my face into the soft tendrils of her short blond hair, sniffing up the scent of wind and a sweet, carefree smell which resembled grass. I smiled and rocked her some more until the heaviness of her body informed me she was once again asleep. I set her gently on the ground. I lay down next to my sleeping sister. Snuggling closer, I wrapped my arm around the dreaming child and smiled.

The next morning, I set about making breakfast: berries and some cold squirrel meat which I had preserved in long, green leaves. As I unwrapped the squirrel meat, I looked around our small camp, searching for Henry's berries to use in breakfast. *Where could they be?* I realized they were nowhere to be found — and neither was Henry. I took a deep breath and decided not to worry, yet. I would give him ten minutes before I searched for him.

After making a trip to find him, I returned to our site. *Perhaps Henry just got up to relieve himself and is already waiting for me back at camp.* However, when I returned, my stomach fell. He wasn't there.

A note lay on top of Anne's sleeping form, the ink made of berry juice. I sniffed the note and immediately recoiled.

Yes, it was definitely Juji juice — the one Henry had told me was good for writing with but smelled horrible. I hastened to read what the note said. It read,

> Deer Caroline,
> Sory to run owt on you like this but I dydn't tell you becaus I didn't want to leev but my Ma is reel sick with a coff I could not wait another day too riscy thanks for understandeen I left yu a presnt ovur bye Eli
> Henry Williams
> P.S. I'm <u>reel</u> sorry but I had too take the map because I need the munee to git back hom in tyme
> P.P.S. I saw the hole thing last nite and Anne luvs you too Caroline I beleve in you

I reddened. My heart skipped a beat as I read and re-read the words "I believe in you." I cleared my thickening throat.

I paled again as I focused on the more important matters at hand. Henry and the map were both gone; we had no one who knew which food was safe and which wasn't; at least not like Henry. Though I was reluctant to admit it, I was not quite sure where we were, much less where to go from there. I knew the general direction in which we were headed, but a general direction is not enough when one needs to end up in a certain city. I shook my head. *Well, a general direction will have to be enough.*

I found the present Henry left me. It was a couple leaves of the pain-relief plant he had told me about. I picked them up, surprised to find a tear pooling in my eye. *No need to cry,* I commanded. *After all, it was just ol' Henry Williams. Who needs him, anyway.* I took a deep breath and wiped away the tear.

I folded the leaves and put them in the secret pocket inside my dress for later.

Anne's stirring caused me to forget about the leaves I put into my pocket. She stirred from her sleep, murmuring and crying. She rubbed her eyes and sat up.

Since Anne had become accustomed to Henry playing with her first thing each day, this morning she was grumpy. "Boo, where's Henry?" she whined.

"Ssh, don't wake Eli," was my response.

Her voice rose louder. "Where's Henry?" she demanded. She stood up and crossed her arms defiantly.

"He's not here. Now be quiet!" I hissed.

"I don't wanna be quiet, I want Henry!" she shouted. She stamped her foot, then groaned and clutched her stomach. Her face drained of its color. "Boo, my tummy hurts."

I didn't even look at her. "Don't worry. I'm sure it's just a stomach cramp. You may have slept crumpled-up or something." I returned to my thoughts regarding what to do next.

She screamed and stomped her feet.

I started aback, torn out of my thought processes. "Anne! What in the world is the matter?"

She didn't answer but instead kept clutching her stomach and screaming. She grew even paler as she collapsed to the ground.

I rushed to her and knelt at her side. "Anne, are you alright? I — I mean, I'm sure you are, but, uh, this... this is…" I quit talking, not wanting to frighten her further. Her sudden silence disturbed me.

I felt her pulse, which was irregular. Instead of the normal *THUMP-thump-thump*, it was faster and skipped a beat every now and again, like *THUMP-thumpthump…thump*. I then started checking her stomach. I brushed my fingers over her abdomen. "Does this hurt?" I started to say.

She screamed in answer and then convulsed. "I'm gonna…" she said. Her face told me the rest of the message.

I jumped out of the way in time to avoid the vomit. She sat on her hands and knees. Her stomach's reaction rocked her little body until she collapsed and rolled onto her back, coughing and crying. I put her head in my lap and wiped her mouth with a large leaf.

"It's alright," I whispered, stroking her hair to calm her down, "it's alright. Ssh, ssh, ssh… you're alright. You're alright. You're going to be fine."

My hands trembled as I rocked her. I prayed God would forgive me for making her a promise I couldn't keep.

She continued to cry for half an hour or so, which woke Eli.

He groaned and turned over, staring at us. "What's —" he started, pointing at the hysterical Anne.

I shook my head and put a finger to my lips and he let his sentence trail off. He stood up and came over to me, leaning down to whisper to me.

"What under the sun?" he asked.

"I have no idea. She just woke up, said her stomach hurt, and then she threw up. She's been crying and screaming since."

He bit the edge of his lip and muttered, "Hm." There was silence until he continued in a happy, sing-song voice, "Anne, do you want to —"

But the attention given her caused her to scream louder. He covered his ears and pointed to the trees, shouting to me he'd be right back. I nodded. Meantime, I kept stroking her hair and whispering little comforts meant nothing.

But even as I told her not to worry, I panicked in my mind. What was this thing had invaded my beloved sister's body? Would she recover? Was it contagious? Was it temporary? Surely she wouldn't die.

Right?

My hands grew clammy. Or would she? Was this... this whatever it was... was it deadly? And if it was fatal, was there a cure? There were so many questions with so few answers.

So I did the best I could. I gave my lap for a pillow, a drink of water when she needed it (frequently, I found), and a stomach rub when it was cramped up. But I knew, though her comfort was a priority right now, our journey was the priority in the grand scheme of things. It was fine with me if she needed one, two, or maybe even three days to relax and get it back together, but I knew we had to keep moving. If she was dying that would be one thing, but a simple case of diarrhea—or whatever she had—was another.

I moved our camp to under the cover of the trees, where we would be safer from the animals living in fields, things like venomous snakes, mice, chiggers, and vultures. Two days and two nights passed in the same routine. We woke at around four in the morning and Anne would be in extreme pain until she relieved herself. Then she'd attempt to force down some breakfast before vomiting it up, along with anything she had tried to force down in the last ten hours. For the next two hours, she'd lie groaning and sobbing on the ground while Eli and I took turns comforting her. Then she'd be so dehydrated she could barely talk, and we'd force some water in her. Then the entire thing would repeat.

By the third morning, we were both tired — in fact, bone-dead exhausted would be a better description. At four we rose to the now-familiar sound of Anne screaming. Bags drooped beneath our purple eyes, and our joints creaked and groaned as we dragged them off of the hard ground. However, as bad as we looked, Anne looked worse.

Days earlier, Anne had been a cheerful, fat, healthy toddler with thick, shiny skin, perhaps weighing fifty pounds. But now, her skin was shriveled and turning an odd blue color, her eyes were bulging out of their sockets, she had bags under her eyes an inch long, and she had lost a noticeable amount of weight in just two days. She was lethargic, never rising except to vomit, drink water, or go to the bathroom.

When I encouraged her to get up and walk around with me, her eyes grew large with horror and she told me it hurt, it will hurt, it did hurt. My sight grew blurry with tears as I stared at her agony and condition. At the age of four, she was experiencing more pain, more hurt, more fear than perhaps I had ever felt at once. And she was afraid, yes, but not as afraid as I was for by the second night, I knew what was attacking her. Given the symptoms, I could tell she had the Asiatic Cholera, a disease that invades those who have drunk dirty water or who have touched the waste of those who have it. The disease, whose main symptom is severe diarrhea, kills within five days, and two days already passed. Anne had three days, including today, to live.

Knowing this, I cleaned up her vomit, rubbed her cramping, agonized stomach when she wanted me to, helped her get privacy to go to the bathroom the twelve or so times a day it was necessary, and whispered her to sleep every night. When she could force something down, I gave her stewed nuts and baked apples which I cooked throughout the day on the surface of a temporary pot made of a curved stone.

I didn't dare share the horrible awareness, for fear Eli would feel the same heartache I did. It was a burden... no, more like a staggering weight, to be alone in the knowledge of and therefore unable to discuss what I knew was coming: Anne's imminent death. Knowing, but not being able to tell, was enough to drive me mad. I tried to ease the pain of the knowledge by throwing myself into her comfort.

These were my thoughts as we started the third day. By morning, she grew worse. She floated in and out of consciousness. Whenever she was awake she was screaming. How she had the energy to do that, I don't know. I kept track of how many times I took her to the bathroom eighteen: times back and forth, back and forth. All day long, it seemed, we were either walking to or from the spot we designated for her to go, or I was helping her while there. Careful, of course. It would do no one any good if I were to catch the disease as well. By five o'clock at night, she passed out in my arms, her limbs hanging below her and her head hung limp from her tiny neck. Eli asked if he could take a nap; as tired as the poor thing was I gave him permission.

I gathered Anne a little closer in my arms and stared at her. Everything zoomed into reality. This was no game. Anne was dying. Seized with a fit of passion, I brought her close to my shoulder and squeezed the little girl as if I never would again. I wept on her back, while her head now rested on my shoulder, rocking back and forth in an effort to control my emotions. She felt so frail, so fragile, so weak in my arms I was afraid to touch her. Afraid if I squeezed harder, she would shatter into a thousand glass fragments, which could never be picked up and put together again. *We have two nights left to spend with her.*

I laid her on the ground next to me. Breathing heavy with concern, I tried to quiet myself lest I wake up Eli or, worse, Anne herself, with my crying. The last thing I wanted to do was upset Anne in her… in her last days. Even before this thought was over, however, I fell into a fresh fit of sobbing. I closed my eyes to steady my emotions, snuggled close to Anne, and began praying out of habit.

"God, please help Anne. Please, please, help Anne. God, please help…" They were the only words coming into my mind. I'm sure He knew what I meant.

I soon fell into a turbulent sleep.

On the last of Anne's two days I felt miserable. I was exhausted, heartbroken, and unsure of what to do to help her. I lost hope as well. I saw things with a realistic view. She was going to die, and I couldn't stop it.

However, I have a mighty God. In the midst of a hopeless situation, God in His mercy reminded me He is more powerful than I could know.

I did not hear the cry I heard every morning for the last three days. I rolled over. Exhaustion caused such a state of mental shutdown I went back to sleep. When I awoke the sun was high in the sky.

I gasped and jumped up. I ran to Anne. She lay on the ground on her back, listless, pale, and much too silent. My eyes widened… "Anne! I screamed. I shook her. My heart was in my throat. Tears already blurred my vision. *Please, God, no…*

She didn't stir.

After a heart-stopping moment, she spoke. "Boo, stop shaking me," she moaned. She yawned and rubbed her eyes. "Will you take me to go to the bathroom?"

I broke down into laughter of relief. I pressed her body to mine. "Of course I will, darling," I whispered. I kissed her dry forehead. "Of course." I swooped her up into my arms and walked towards the forest.

"Boo, put me down," she protested.

I did as she directed. She offered me her hand. Hand in hand, she and I walked with no crying out. Without being carried, she walked to the spot, completed her business, and walked back to the clearing, where Eli was still sleeping.

She plopped down on the ground and started playing with a piece of grass, making them interact like she would have if in perfect health. Perplexed at her behavior, I leaned down and woke up Eli to get his opinion. I winced in guilt. He needed his sleep.

He dragged open his eyelids and groaned as he stood. "Okay, I'm up," he moaned.

I shook my head and put my finger to my lips. He arched his eyebrows. I pointed in Anne's direction. She was played in a beam of sunlight, laughing and having fun with her dolly.

He cocked his head. "What...?" he started.

I shrugged. "I was praying last night—" I whispered.

That was explanation enough for him; he interrupted me. "Me too!"

We stared at her in amazed silence.

I took Anne to the bathroom six times that day. In fact, she went by herself twice toward the end of the day, so technically I took her four times. She ate. Not a lot, but she ate. Furthermore, she kept her food down. Encouraged by this improvement, I gave her as much water as I could get her to drink. She vomited once in the mid-afternoon, so I toned down the water-giving. She did not throw up again. I even got a chance to take a bath. A — luxury not experienced for several days.

That night I pondered the drastic difference in my mood. Whereas the night before, I was sobbing, exhausted, dirty, tired, and unhopeful, this night, I felt refreshed, joyful at her speedy and divine recovery, and clean. Hope remained.

The fifth morning, I woke at five, ready to doctor Anne. To my amazement she was not awake. She slept for another five hours. Since I knew rest was essential to a quick and complete recovery, I left Anne sleeping...and sleeping... and sleeping. I sat on the ground staring at the two sleeping children for hours. After what seemed an eternity of waiting, I decided sleeping that long was just plain lazy, so I woke them up. Eli apologized for sleeping so late, but Anne needed the rest to fight the disease, so I allowed her to go back to sleep. *If she needs to sleep so long in order to make herself healthy, then so be it.*

Eli and I remained by ourselves the rest of the day. Anne slept through breakfast, lunch, and almost through dinner. She awoke as we started to eat.

Finding herself ravenous with hunger, Anne ate the portion of squirrel meat I had set aside for her.

"Boo, I'm still hungry," she said.

"Here, have mine," I said, surprised. I handed her my plate.

She devoured it. "Boo, I'm still hungry," she repeated.

Eli and I exchanged shocked looks. "Here, have mine too," he answered. He handed her his plate as well.

I shook my head at the peculiarity of it all. After she ate all of our food, Anne fell back asleep. I woke her only once, to drink some water.

I reckoned the time arrived to move on. Eli and I could take turns carrying Anne; she was now healthy enough to move. I nodded. The next morning, we would be on our way. "Anne, are you ready to go?" I coaxed.

"Yup!" she answered.

She skipped ahead.

"Anne, come back. I'm going to carry—" I cut myself off and shrugged. If she could and wanted to walk, then so be it. I noticed her normal weight returning, and her skin was back to its white tint, the bags under her eyes disappearing. She was recovering; it was not just hopeful thinking.

All day we traveled. Anne's recovery slowed us down, however, so we made eight miles.

Later that night, we came upon a forest. Anne and Eli were trailing behind me, complaining their small feet were throbbing. I didn't disagree with them. I could hardly keep my eyes open in the fading twilight. We found a glen and stopped for the night. We all cuddled up on a bed of cushy pine needles, our body warmth keeping us comfortable. I was just drifting off when I heard someone talking. My eyes shot wide awake. I looked from side to side and realized it was Eli. I smiled.

"Purple Retrievers," he murmured. His eyes were closed.

"Purple Retrievers?" I repeated.

"Mm-hmm," he answered.

Anne grinned at me. I smiled too. I knew what was coming—one of our favorite games to play with Eli.

"Well, where did you get the purple Retrievers?" I asked.

He took a deep breath and talked again in a dreamy voice. "Michigan," he said.

"Michigan?"

"Yep."

I made up another question to keep him going. "How much did they cost?"

"Five."

"Five what?"

"Five... hours."

"Five hours?"

"Yep," he said, with a seriousness in his voice. "What are you going to do with the purple Retrievers?"

"Ride them."

I smiled. "Ride them? To where?"

"Michigan."

I bit my lip to hold back my laughter. I didn't want to wake him. "Ah, Michigan again. Why Michigan? What's so important there?"

He sighed. "Caroline," he said condescendingly. Anne laughed. "Cookbooks," he replied.

"I see. So what you're saying is you want to ride the purple Retrievers to Michigan so you can...." I stifled a laugh. "So you can buy cookbooks?"

He nodded. My cheeks were red with the effort of keeping in a laugh and I couldn't contain it any longer. I let out a burst of laughter and his eyelids flew open. Anne was rolling on the ground laughing, her hands holding her stomach. I tried to hold myself up as I squeezed my eyes closed, unable to breathe because I was laughing so hard.

"Aw, man, you were doing it again, weren't you?" Eli complained.

I nodded, running out of breath.

He sighed and shook his head. He glanced in my eyes and after a moment chuckled. Then he laughed. After a moment he joined us in our echoing, breathless laughter.

I stood to walk away, trying to regain my breath and take a break from the painful laughter. I walked outside of the glen and tripped on a branch in the dark.

Someone caught me, and it sure wasn't one of my siblings.

As I turned to see my rescuer, I beheld something that made my heart stop for pure fear. Indians warriors. Everywhere. I opened my mouth to scream, but the one holding me put a strong hand over my mouth, pulling me off the path in one movement. A cloth covered my mouth and nose. He smelled like pine trees and sweat.

I awoke to an aching head and the sound of foreign-sounding voices. I felt groggy and everything felt unreal, like in a dream. I pulled open my tired eyelids and tried to examine my surroundings, but couldn't for the utter darkness. The air felt hot and stuffy. I made my headache worse by trying to remember where I was. The last thing I remembered, Anne was sick. *No, that was days ago.* I concentrated harder, frowning. *Oh yes — the last thing I remember; I was walking along the path when something scared me. But what—*

My thoughts cleared and I realized with a rush of adrenaline my hands were corded to a wooden stake. I was alone in some sort of dwelling. I struggled on the cold ground, yelling for help.

Help came in the form of a huge, bronzed, ripped man who yanked the cloth bag off of my head. He had black hair and wore a traditional outfit of leather pants with a loincloth, but no shirt. I noticed his rippling muscles, but grimaced at how tattoos covered almost every inch of his arms and even his face.

I trembled with the sudden remembrance of Indian "hospitality." Goosebumps raised on my arms. "Wh- what are you doing with me?" I asked. "And who are you? Where are my siblings?" After a moment with no response, I asked, "Don't you speak English?"

"Little English," he replied in a deep, drum-like voice. It had a certain wild sound to it that made me shiver with simultaneous fear and excitement. "I am Crowing Eagle. Take you to Chief."

He walked away, leaving me no plausible choice but to follow him into the darkness outside.

Crowing Eagle led me to meet the "Chief." This gave me a chance to observe the camp. So far I had not seen Eli, but as we twined in between the teepees, I noticed a teepee full of civilized-looking boys and girls huddling around a small fire. *Perhaps he is in there.* For the moment, I was too afraid of Crowing Eagle to interact with him any more than necessary. Maybe I would ask the Chief.

The swift Indian ducked under the flap of the largest teepee I saw on the grounds. I hesitated to follow. But then the smell of hot food caught my nose and I followed him inside.

I came in just in time to see Crowing Eagle touch the Chief's feet and then, bowing, back out of the tent. This left me alone in a tent with the Chief and a very pregnant woman whom I assumed was his wife.

At first, my fear of the people in the tent kept me from noticing anything inside. The Chief stared at me. After a moment my curiosity won over and I feasted my eyes on the sights around me, taking in everything with enthusiasm. There on the floor, on top of an animal skin, lay a feast of sweet potatoes, still-steaming, juicy turkey, buffalo jerky, corn on the cob and corn bread with the butter oozing, vessels of clear, sparkling water, and foods of all other sorts. My mouth watered as I stared at the abundant and extravagant foods.

The Chief spoke breaking silence. I looked in his direction. For a moment, I forgot where I was. "I am Chief Howea of the Sioux tribe. My squaw, Amitola, wishes to keep you as her slave. You will stay either for this purpose or as the wife of one of our braves." He held up his hand in a sign of peace as the color drained from my face. My knees started to buckle under me. Crowing Eagle pulled me back to my feet. "It is either you or your brother, Elijah, who will stay, for Amitola has made known her desire to keep you both. This is a fair offer. You have to choose." He ceased speaking as suddenly as he had begun. He sat statue-like with his legs folded, waiting for my terrible decision.

"Well, sir, the thing of it is," I began.

The pregnant squaw gave me a look of disbelief. A look of disbelief and anger. I shrank back from the pair, terrified. *What had I done wrong?*

A terrible look in the Chief's eyes froze me in place, wondering yet again what I had done wrong. In my panicked state of mind, I rushed through everything I saw and what I did so far. In a flashback of memory, I saw Crowing Eagle bow and touch the Chief's feet before speaking. Perhaps I was supposed to imitate the action as well. I hoped the act served as common courtesy and was not a privilege of some sort. I touched his feet, and backed away, hoping my deed would prove acceptable. He nodded in approval and some of his rigidity evaporated. I sighed.

"Sir — Chief, I mean — if it pleases you, may I think about it?"

"You have seven suns until the choice is no longer yours," he replied.

Crowing Eagle now appeared behind me. When the Chief waved his hand, Crowing Eagle "escorted" me out; in other words, he picked me up and carried me over his shoulder like so many buffalo skins.

"Where are you taking me?" I demanded, bumping against his back.

He did not reply but instead dumped me inside the teepee where I had seen the other non-Indian children. He closed the flap after me. I studied my surroundings. Five children stared back, evaluating me. They soon became bored and turned back to the elderly Indian sitting in the middle of the tent. Neither Eli nor Anne was among them. I tried to think where they could be.

My stomach dropped. Surely they would have taken them too and not just left them alone to... No. No, they must have taken them too. Not even wild men are so cruel. I wiped my palms on my skirt and took a deep breath to steady my stomach.

The man proceeded with a story in perfect English. I sat down in the circle and tried to look like I was paying attention instead of planning mine and my sibling's escapes. When he finished with, "and that is how the stars came to twinkle so," all the children jumped up and hugged him.

One small boy about six years old cried, "Oh, thank you, Papa Indie! Tell us another one, please?"

All of the others joined in a chorus of 'please.' "No, I don't think so. Young ones need rest, just as the sun rests every night." He tousled the boy's thick black hair.

All of the children groaned as he stood up and left the teepee. As he passed me, I caught his robe and stopped him. I remembered to be respectful and touch his feet before I spoke, hoping the gesture would cancel out the rudeness of my grabbing his robe.

"Sir — my brother, Eli and my sister, Anne. Where are they?" I asked simply.

"They are in the other tent," he replied. His apparent kindness kept him from getting angry at me for touching his robe, although he did edge the fabric out of my sweaty and clammy hands. He walked away.

I scrambled after him. "What other tent? Why?"

One of the girls in the circle piped up. "So we don't plan with our siblings to run away," she said, laughing.

I turned back to the Indian, but he was gone.

I groaned and fell to the floor. I had to find a way to get to Eli and Anne. Otherwise, one of us would be chosen in seven days. As this thought came to me, I reviewed my choices, half of me panicking and the other half of me knowing I had to stay calm. I paced the dirt floor. The other children watched me with curbed interest. *Option number one; if I choose to give up Eli — No. I will not lose one more person. Whatever it takes.*

The only option left meant I became a slave. Eli and Anne would have to go on without me. I hesitated. It's possible to survive, but without anyone else to help them find food, or a safe place to sleep, or to find their way when they're lost... the chances are remote. And if I don't choose in seven days, one of those options will be chosen anyway. I moaned and sunk down into an uncomfortable, hunched-over position facing the teepee wall.

"Caroline!" a voice hissed.

"Leave me alone," I moaned.

The owner of the voice shook me. "Ssh! It's Eli. Be quiet!"

I twisted around. "Eli! You don't belong in here —"

He cut me off short. "I know that, but..." he shrugged and made a twisted face. "Does it matter?" I nodded, conceding his point. He continued. "Now. Which one of us is going to stay?"

I turned to face him. "The Chief talked to you, too, then?"

"Yes, he told me about it the other morning. How could they do such a thing?" He shook his head.

"Wait... 'the other morning?'" My stomach fell for another time that day. "Elijah, what's today?"

"By the phase of the moon, I think it's September 21st. And before you panic, I left Anne in the other teepee, sleeping. She's fine, not sick anymore; the only way you can tell she was sick in the first place her eyes are different, if you know what I mean." I nodded; I knew exactly what he was talking about. I had seen the same thing in his eyes. "She's happy, though, and keeps playing with her dolly," he continued.

I smiled. My face crinkled with all the dried dust and sweat and tears. "Good. I'm glad she's happy, even during this chaos. At least she'll go free..." I sighed.

"What?" he asked, startled.

"I said at least she'll be free." One of the children next to me groaned and rolled over. We lowered our voices to a whisper.

He sighed, mixing his breath with the wind of the night. "I see the Chief didn't tell you everything. One of us will stay with the Indians to be... to be Amitola's slave, right?" he asked. I nodded, wincing. "Okay. That one will go through a special acceptance ceremony and the others may, or may not go free. The acceptance ceremony should be easy for you. They don't seem to think of girls as very important. You only stand in the middle of a ring and let a bunch of squaws dance around you. Then you'll be one of them forever…" He didn't say *Whether you like it or not.* He cleared his throat. "But for me, since I'm a boy, it'd be much harder.

"I'd have to pass five tests to prove my worthiness as a brave before I could be… accepted."

"Even as a slave?"

He nodded and continued. "First I'd have to make myself a bow and arrow set without help.

"Then I'd have to catch and kill a deer with my bare hands. Which, of course, is provided I can sneak up to it quiet enough.

"The third test should be interesting. I have to catch a wild horse and ride it without a saddle across the plains to the North."

I opened my mouth to speak but he held up his hand.

"Then, for the fourth test, I'd have to be so swift-footed I can make my way past a line of Indian braves."

I interrupted. "Well… at least that one doesn't sound too hard…" A little spark of hope burst to life in my heart, desperate as it was.

He replied, "They'd be throwing spears when I pass. The test is to make it past them… alive."

I recoiled. My brain just seemed to shut down in emotional breakdown. "No, no no," I muttered, "This is all wrong. They can't. No, no no!"

Elijah waited out my rant. "Caroline, it's alright," he said.

I lifted my hands from my face. "Eli, I don't know how to get us out of here! I don't know… I've never been taught…"

He sandwiched my hands in his. "Caroline, Caroline," he soothed. "It's alright, okay? You and Anne are going to be just fine."

"How do you know?" I muttered.

He let out a long sigh, the kind that wells from deep within. "If I have any ounce of control in this, I swear you and Anne will be alright."

I nodded. "Alright, okay. Maybe you're right."

He stared into my eyes. "I am."

I took a deep breath and nodded again, accepting his comfort. "Wait…" I tried to concentrate. Something didn't seem right. He shifted uncomfortably. "Elijah… you weren't planning on staying… were you?"

He looked away. "Caroline, I want you and Anne to get out of here. An Indian camp is no place for you. There's no kind of life here for a good Christian girl, and certainly for no sister of mine."

"Well, it's no kind of life for you either! Eli… what are we supposed to do?" I searched his gaze, looking for an answer. "I don't know. We just have to hold out hope some outside source will change our circumstances. Caroline, you need to be prepared for the possibility we won't all make it out of this."

The frankness of this statement shocked me. I knew it all along, but hearing Eli say it was a lot worse than I imagined. "Sure we can!" I stuttered.

"Caroline, you know we can't. Let's not pretend. There's no use for that here." He sat back, leaning on his arms.

I heard a rustling outside. I saw the flap being lifted open. Eli and I fell to the ground. He scooched as close as he could to the teepee wall to become inconspicuous.

The Indian went to the other side of the teepee first to check on those children. I closed my eyes, still trembling but hoping against hope he wouldn't notice. Eli did the same, lying on his side and quivering. The one named Biting Snake came to our feet and looked us over. I tried to control my trembling, worried the darkness was not dark enough to mask the tell-tale signs we were up to something.

He stepped over me and leaned closer to Eli.

He grabbed his shoulder and started to roll him over to see his face.

I heard the Chief call something in a foreign tongue.

Biting Snake made his way out of the teepee.

Eli and I opened our eyes, staring at each other with wide eyes and shaking hands.

"That was too close," Eli whispered.

Alexander

FIVE DAYS LATER, as I lay down to sleep, Eli tapped my shoulder in the pitch black night. He leaned down and whispered into my ear so quiet I almost couldn't hear him.

"Caroline!"

He wriggled down where I lay and snuggled against me so it wouldn't look like two separate people.

"Who's going to stay?" he asked.

Day six of the same discussion. I felt hardened to it. "I think I should."

The conversation took a quick turn from the norm when he replied, "I agree. So the morning after next, when they come to ask who's staying, you're going to tell them it's you."

"Uh… yes, I suppose so!" I was caught off guard by his quick decision. "Eli —?"

"Yes?" He responded a little too quickly.

An Indian poked his head into the teepee. Eli and I flattened out on the floor and tried to look like we were asleep. After the fifth night, I got better at mimicking sleep. It comes easily when your life depends on it. After a moment, we were in the clear again.

"Never mind. We shouldn't talk more than necessary. Let's talk in the morning instead. I love you." I ruffled his long, tangled hair, becoming curly after months of not being cut.

"O.K. I love you too, Caroline." He hugged me. He stood and picked his way out of the teepee. His face shone pale in the moonlight as he checked for guards. And then he was gone as swiftly as he came.

The next morning, I stood still and quiet as an Indian tied me to a horse so I would walk beside it. As his rough hands touched my wrist, tying it to the rope, my mind couldn't help but wonder if I was destined to become his bride. I turned away in disgust. I heard Anne, screaming and thrashing. Someone set her on the same horse to which I was attached and tied her to the saddle.

"Give it back!" she screamed.

"Anne, quiet," I urged.

She sobbed in reply.

"Anne, tell me what's wrong. I can't help you if you don't tell me what's wrong!"

She attempted to explain in a hysterical, slurred wail.

"Anne, calm down, okay? You have to—" I changed tactics. "Ssh, ssh, it's okay, sweetie. It's okay." I ignored the rope biting into my wrists as I stretched as far as I could reach to pat her leg. She calmed to a hyperventilating sniffle. "Alright now," I soothed. "Tell me what's the matter.""M...my...d..doll...dolly... i..iiss... goooonnee!" she wailed. After exclaiming such tragic news to me, she broke out afresh in sobs.

"Sssh," I said, looking around to see who was displeased by her loud and annoying screams. I continued to stroke her leg in order to quiet her, but she paid no attention and the rope was turning my wrists red with the effort, so I stopped trying.

"I wouldn't complain if I were you," one of the girls named Annemarie, tartly interrupted.

"Oh, what do you know? You're not me, so don't act like you know what I should do." I turned back to Anne, ignoring Annemarie's gasp of fake shock. While looking behind me in a desperate attempt to see if she dropped it, my sight was drawn to a bag roped to the side of a horse about fifteen feet behind me. There was only one object pushing the top of the leather sack open: the doll.

"Stop your foolishness!" Biting Wolf commanded.

Anne's eyes widened. She wailed louder. By this time the other children were stirring. Everyone was staring and some of the other Indians were coming over to intervene.

"Make her stop!" he directed at me.

"I can't!"

"You must," he said darkly.

I gulped.

"She will stop if she gets her dolly," I shouted over the noise of her screams.

"Make her stop now!" he shouted. I jumped as he raised his voice.

"I—I don't think I can," I squeaked.

He leaned down towards my level. His wild breath clouded around my face. "If you wish to stay in place of your brother," he replied in response to my anxious pleadings, "you must prove yourself worthy to care for the children. So make her stop. Now."

The threat was real now. The color drained from my face. "Anne, please," I pleaded. "Be brave, okay? Be brave for John?"

She nodded and wiped her nose on the back of her hand. My heart grew a little more even. I took a deep breath to calm my nerves.

After a moment my stomach twisted with dread as I saw her throw a forlorn glance back at the doll. Sure enough, the sniffling and whimpering started again. She sat on the horse, her head bowed and her back slumped over. She cried without making a sound, every now and then emitting a whine. Soon the sound was grating on my nerves, but I steeled my stomach to deal with it. But after a while, the mere thought of the sounds drove me to gnashing my teeth. For forty minutes these sounds went on until I felt I could no longer stand it, no matter what Biting Wolf said about it.

"Sir, she has to have that doll," I said, almost begging him. He gave me no reply but a stoic face. "It's not yours! You can't just take it from her!"

He beckoned to the man behind him, the one carrying the doll.

I sighed with relief.

I should have known better. Biting Wolf pulled the doll out of the sack and thrust it toward Anne. She reached for it with an ecstatic smile and a giggle. Just before her pudgy hands grasped the doll, Biting Wolf threw it on the ground. Anne's jaw dropped. She put her hands over her mouth and her whole body shook. With wide eyes she watched in horror as he guided the horse to trample on the doll. Its hooves stomped on the china face. Anne and I gasped. We saw a last view of her beloved doll's face crushed inwards, its beautiful smile turned in upon itself in a grotesque imitation of what it had been. The doll lay on the ground, sprawled out with mangled limbs and a broken, flat face.

"How could you?" I demanded, crying for Anne's sake.

"My dollyyyy!" she wailed with the guttural sound of a heart being broken.

"May that be a lesson," he responded.

With no choice, we rode on to wherever they were going to take us. I couldn't help myself but took one last look at the doll through the tears, exhaustion and distress. I made no move to stifle my tears until Biting Wolf told me he would not tolerate tears either. In fear, I stopped.

The rest of the day the fear remained and I didn't speak, lest I be accused of plotting. I dared hold a conversation with Eli only once, when we stopped for our daily meal. In near-silent whispers we spoke of things too serious for our young minds to ponder. Things that would make an adult quake with fear. Things no child should ever have to know. We talked of the separation of our family.

We wolfed down the crumbs they gave us, and I overheard one Indian tell another our group walked or rode twenty miles that day. By my calculations, that meant our camp was about thirty miles from Springfield, Illinois.

"Up!" one of the men barked. I sighed and stood to my feet, wincing at the throbbing in my blistering, swollen feet. I wished the trip would be over—and they would take me wherever they were going. But then I wondered if I truly wanted it to be over. I threw a glance back at Eli and allowed myself to imagine what life would be like never seeing him again. I pressed my lips together to prevent the sigh escaping them.

I heard one of the braves announce something to the Chief in a silvery tongue which I did not understand. All I could distinguish was the word "Krueger," and then I heard a muffled sound.

Chief Howea nodded. He spurred his horse to trot faster. Our heels were whipped, forcing us to walk double time. I tried to ignore the streaks of blood on the ground left by those in front of me. I attempted to put the pain out of my mind by concentrating on something else.

First of all, who or what were the Kruegers? I heard the Indians saying this name frequently. I wore myself out thinking until I realized it didn't matter; whether they were evil or do-gooders, my approach toward them would not be stopped. I put the unpleasant thought out of my mind and concentrated on another problem.

At sunrise of the next day, Anne and I would have to say goodbye to our brother forever as he left to complete the journey. I planned out how I was going to comfort her. I knew singing almost always made her feel better, so— My thoughts were cut off with a cold jolt of adrenaline as I realized the Chief said nothing about Anne staying. Only myself. Anne was going with Eli, leaving me alone. My heart sunk within me.

When we could snatch a moment to discuss our plight in miniscule voices, Eli and I did not seem to be able to bring ourselves to talk about the one thing we needed to — our goodbyes. I just did not know what to say, because nothing seemed adequate. What one phrase could I say to mean 'Goodbye forever?' I hardly thought 'it's been great' was adequate.

As we made camp for the night I took the chance to go relieve myself. I did this to get away from my captors for a moment and perhaps get a moment to think. However, crushing my dream, a squaw volunteered to go with me in order to make sure I didn't run away. We tramped away into the forest. I came to a secluded place.

I sat down, put my forehead on my knees, and prayed. I lifted my gaze to the silvery moon through the dark branches. "Father," I started, whispering, "as King David wrote, 'Help me, O LORD my God! Save me because of Your unfailing love.' Please, show me the way to save what is left of my family. Please, Jesus, I need you. Help the

Indians to do what's right. Please settle my stomach. Help me figure out what to do and give me the ability and resources to do it, if it's in Your will. Amen."

The breeze whispered in my ear; He heard my pleas. I felt a cradle in the cold, an embrace in the wind. I smiled, my spirit lifted by the broken light of the white moon.

Feeling more hopeful, I stood and saw a sign with writing on it. It read, 'New Salem — 8 miles to the North' with an arrow pointing to the right. My eyes teared up. God gave me a way to save all of us. Staring at the place where I fell to my knees in prayer a moment earlier, I knew He helped.

"Thank you, Father," I whispered.

Just then the squaw ran up. "Come now," she said gruffly. She made her way through the vines and bushes. I followed, smiling because I knew my God could see me.

I awoke to a warm, sunny day. However, my waking was not such a sunny affair. I was yanked to my feet, as my eyelids flew open.

"Come," Biting Snake ordered.

He took my arm and commenced to drag me toward the dreaded horse. "Let me go!" I yelled, still trying to blink the bleariness out of my eyes.

He kept walking, undaunted. "It is time," he said.

"Time? Time for what?" My heart stopped. A rush of adrenaline went to my head.

"For your brother to leave."

"Wait!" He slowed down. "Take me to Chief Howea. I have chosen."

He complied, still dragging me across the rough ground. When we got to the tent Biting Snake all but threw me in. He left to collect the other children for departure. I approached the Chief, who was busy threading glass beads onto his feather headdress. I huffed and massaged my aching back. After a moment I approached and touched Howea's feet, very much irritated.

"Alright. I've chosen."

"Speak," he said, not even looking at me. He didn't care about the fate of my family, not even enough to look up from threading his beads. It made me sick. I looked away.

I steadied my trembling voice and heart. "Me."

"What do you have to offer for this change?"

What? "Ah, I'm sorry, sir. I don't think I understand."

"Your brother has already traded us the doll and himself in exchange for your and your sister's freedom. What is your offer?"

Dots swam before my eyes. "That — that's impossible," I stuttered. My face was a pasty white.

He remained calm as he continued to thread beads onto his turkey-feather headdress. "It is not impossible," he said.

"But… I'll never see him again," I whispered to myself.

His Indian ears picked up the noise. "I see you have no other offer. Chaska!" He snapped his fingers.

Chaska, a burly member of the Indian group, entered the tent to take me away. I cried, "Please! At least let Anne and me say goodbye!"

He continued threading, his ears closed to my tearful pleas.

Chaska picked me up and carried me off, still screaming, to his horse. It was when I ran out of breath I stopped wailing. He set Anne on my lap, and he tied her onto my waist. I tried to jump off but he had already tied us both onto the animal. I writhed, trying to loosen my bonds. I threw a forlorn glance in the direction of the others. Suddenly, to my dismay and hope, Eli emerged from the children's' teepee. He ran to the horse and caught my tied hand. The touch of his hand burned into my flesh.

With a look of burden in his young eyes, he whispered, "Caroline, I'm so sorry. I had to trick you to get you free." A small smile grew across his tender face, tempered by the tears on his face. "But now they're letting you go!" he said in a small voice.

"Eli, no, please, I don't want you to do this! Don't leave me, please," I wept.

He spoke over my pleas. "I love you both. Always remember me, and Anne, obey Caroline—"

My moan spiraled out in the glen. "Elijah, I swear this isn't the end! I will find you, and everything will be okay..." I hung my head, the hot tears running down onto my neck. "Eli, why would you deceive me like this? You're going to be killed!"

"You know I have even less chance of making it alive in the forest." He added a squeeze to my hand. "You can do it, Caroline." He stared into my eyes, his gaze flicking back and forth between my eyes. "I know it."

Chaska mounted his horse and yelled for it to go. He dug his heels into the black sides of the horse, making it start to whinny and trot forwards. Eli gave my hand a final squeeze then dropped it as we separated forever.

"Eli, no!" I screamed. I struggled through my tears against my bonds.

"Goodbye! Goodbye!" he yelled. His diminishing figure was waving for as long as I could see it.

When I could no longer distinguish him from the green trees surrounding the camp, I hung my head and sobbed. My stomach racked with pain and my lungs gasping for breath, I turned and vomited. Chaska noticed but did not stop.

"Serves you right for all of your complaining," I heard the little girl on my right, Annemarie, mutter. I stared at her with a fury radiating from my body. She backed down after a moment and turned away.

I wiped off my mouth, dried my tears on my shoulder, and said not a word. In my silence I was more fearful, for there was a madness growing against its constraint. My mind was boiling with desperate planning. *It is time for a level head. If we are all going to make it out of this alive, then I must come up with a plan.*

The thoughts rushed through my head at a thousand miles an hour. I wondered; did they deceive Eli? Would they let us go free? After all, why would they? When they could gain so much by not letting us go free, why would they give up such a precious prize? Eli's kind and noble sacrifice, wasted! If only he knew his surrender gained nothing! My hand clenched into a fist. I soon felt the blood trickle down my hands where my fingernails had pierced them. I took a deep breath to calm myself and continued planning our escape.

In my desperation I remembered the sign I had seen. If there were people to help me eight miles away, then they'd be close enough to help if we were traveling in their direction. The sign said north… and judging by the sun, we were either going north or south. And so I prayed we were going north. What else could I do? Next step—I needed a distraction. What could I do to escape from the Kruegers and from the Indians at the same time? I needed to catch the attention of people nearby. People who could rid me of both our enemies. Maybe a loud noise? No. The distraction would last a moment. I needed something more permanent—something to bring the von Kruegers to a halt and cause the Indians to leave us. Maybe if the Indians thought there's a threat to themselves, they would leave us. What fear could I generate and control to scare a whole group of Indians? An animal? No, I couldn't control an animal big enough to frighten the steady nerves of an Indian.

Aha! I straightened up and smiled for the first time in a long time. My confidence grew the more I thought about my new plan. If I turned the von Kruegers against the Indians, then they would distract each other; in the chaos I could get help to rescue Eli! I grinned and began to put more detail into the plan.

Before we had gone on long, perhaps about seven miles, we slowed. It looked like we were approaching our destination. I craned my head around Chaska to see what "our destination" was like.

In a small glen sat a petite brick house. The brick was painted white and the door-jam black. It was an abandoned house; the flowers out front were wilting, the front windows were clouded, the roof was green with mold, and the door was broken.

Chaska jumped from the horse and began to untie me. Holding me with one hand on my raggedy braid and one hand on Anne's arm, he led me into what I expected to be a worn-down, rotting, old house.

The sight I met was the opposite. My mouth flew open as I was pushed through the house. Hanging from the newly-painted ceiling was a glass chandelier, which threw the light of many candles around the lavish room. Peeking out from behind the door sat a velvet rug. A golden candle-plate sat on top of the brand new piano in the hall. As I looked down at my feet I recognized an ornamental, hand-woven rug softening the sounds of our feet.

Behind one of the doors we passed, I saw five Indian braves sitting tied to chairs, gagged but still retaining a proud face. They were sitting ramrod-straight and staring straight ahead. I understood why we had come here; the Indians wanted to exchange us for their braves.

Anne and I were led along with several other children into the next room. I gasped in awe. *How can they afford all this?* I wondered. Windows opened up the large room on the side of the house, giving it a fresh, natural feel. Outside I saw the swaying leaves of green trees and the shimmering of the blue sky. The long, lush grass emitted relaxation, a luxury I had not been able to afford for many a week. Sunlight filtered through the spotless glass of the windows, dancing on the table and contrasting with the man who turned to greet us.

He was wearing all black and was well over six feet tall. His moustache was long and groomed, the slick black hairs brushed into exact place. There was a sadistic gleam in his eyes as he stated, "Sit."

He beckoned to the long, black table, flanked by beautiful wooden chairs. I glanced around the room, waiting for him to tell me where to sit.

After a short silence, Annemarie voiced everyone's thoughts, asking, "Where?"

"Sit," he repeated.

Not about to rebel against this powerful-looking stranger, we stumbled round the table, confused. Eventually we arranged ourselves and watched him. Anne sat, cowering, at my side. Her eyes wide in fear, she clung to my arm. The man dismissed the Indians and they walked outside. I watched them through the windows.

"Children," he announced, "you will be treated this fine morning to a large dish of ice-cream."

We all looked at each other for a silent moment, not believing in our good luck. We broke into relieved cheers. After all, chocolate ice-cream was my favorite treat! Anne did not cheer. She still clung to my arm, unmoving.

Almost as soon as the man had announced this delicacy, five people came into the room. They all dressed identically, with white shirts whose sleeves reached their elbow. Two of them were men—the other three were older boys. They each carried tubs of ice-cream and lined up in a perfect line without a word.

"This is James."

With a proud nod of his head, one of the two adults introduced himself. He was a skinny man wearing a large, Texas-style hat. He sneered at us.

"This is Charlie," he said next.

One of the younger ones, a nervous-looking boy with a mop of red hair and a face full of freckles, bowed then stood again.

"This is Bram,"

The other adult, a heavy-set man with scars all across his body, turned his nose up at us and drew himself up to his full height.

"And these two are Kenneth and Alexander."

Kenneth was a chubby boy of about fifteen. His thick pink cheeks were wrinkled with signs of vigorous exercise and he had clear scars on his arms and hands. He happened to glance over at me, and, seeing me staring at the scars, hid them behind his back and turned a deep red. He turned his gaze to stare straight ahead.

I looked at Alexander. I raised an eyebrow; he was a good-looking young man. He was about six feet tall, with long perfectly combed brown hair and a sharp, long nose. He had crease lines from lots of laughing, and his lips were upturned in a permanent sort of arrogant smirk. He looked like the sort of fellow one could get to enjoy, someone who could tell a good joke — wait! I ransacked my mind. Why

did he look familiar? I was certain I had seen him
someplace before. I tried to remember.

"Begin," stated the man.

At his word the servers began moving. They set bowls in
front of everyone and then returned to their posts.

"Serve," he commanded next.

I stared at Alexander, trying to place him in my memory.
As I watched him, he came between Anne and I to serve
her the chocolate ice cream and his sleeve slipped up a little.

With a gasp, I saw something I never expected to see
again, — the family birthmark! On the right arm, just
below the elbow, all the Hines used to have a red, berry-
shaped birthmark. Mama did not have it, so all four of us
children had missed out on getting it. In fact, the only child
in the family who did still have it was — Oliver! That's why
he seemed familiar — it was Cousin Oliver! At the sound of
my gasp, "Alexander" straightened up and turned in my
direction. For an infinitesimal second, a flash of recognition
flew across his face. His eyebrows rose as a warning and he
gave a nearly-imperceptible shake of his head.

"What is the matter?" said the man in black. He sounded
quite perturbed.

I realized everyone was looking at me. "Oh — nothing,"
I said, faltering. He continued to glare at me without a
word. "Sir," I added, my face red. He turned back around.

My thoughts raced. *I must speak to Oliver*, I thought as he
gave me a bowl of the chocolaty lusciousness.

I invented a plan.

As he passed me to serve ice cream to Annemarie, who was sitting on my right, I shouted, "Ouch! Get your sleeve out of my hair, gibface," I inclined my head to his arm, pretending my hair was snarled in his sleeve.

He turned to me with a look of surprise. "But... I didn't —" he said with wide eyes.

"Yes, you *did*!" I emphasized, giving him a look. I would've thought he would have caught on by now.

After a moment, he did. "Oh... oh, I'm so sorry! Uh, let me help you." He pretended to fumble around, untangling the nonexistent hair from his sleeve.

"Ouch!" I screamed.

"I'm so sorry, Miss! I —"

Our greeter, who had been getting progressively more and more red-faced, had enough. "Stop! Now!" he roared.

We froze, waiting for him to give us instruction.

"Get up, go in the hallway, figure out this mess, and... don't come back until you're finished!" He lowered his voice to a more smooth and silky tone. "But, Alexander..." he made a threatening face, his eyebrows furrowed and a menacing smile hinting around his lips as he pounded his fist into his open palm discreetly. "Be back quickly."

Oliver blanched and nodded as he replied, "Yes, sir."

We ran into the hallway, my head still inclined in an uncomfortable angle. Oliver closed the door. I laughed and straightened up.

I ran over to him and attempted to throw my arms around him. "Oliver! It's so good to meet you! What have you been doing all these years?"

He put my arms back at their sides. "Caroline, this is no time to reminisce or catch up. We've got to hurry."

I stepped back, aghast at his frankness. "Wait a minute…" Dates flashed through my mind. "How did you know who I am? You left days before I was born. The only way I could recognize you is from a picture we have."

"You don't remember?" He smiled. "They brought me back for three months when you were four." He rolled up his sleeves as he talked.

"What? They did? I don't remember that! Why did you run away again?"

He dismissed my question with a wave of his hand. "A story for another time, but perhaps the tales of my adventures will yet be told you." He flashed the wide grin for which he was famous in our family. I also smiled, though more perhaps at his contagious grin than at his comment.

"Okay, listen. These are very bad people who do very bad things, long story short. You've got to run away, and I'll come with you. Are you alone?"

"Well, no. My sister, Anne, is in there." I pointed back to the room. "But the thing is —" I wrung my hands, afraid to tell him we had to get into the Indian camp.

"What?" he interrupted.

"Well, I kind of already had a plan."

"That's great! So how do we get out?"

"Well, it's not just getting out of here. My brother's… he's in the Indian encampment."

He sighed as he rubbed his temples. After a moment he spoke. "Alright. I think we can pull it off, but it'll require some risks. Are you willing to take on some risks?"

I shrugged. "I have no choice."

This statement did not put him off. "Alright. Here's the plan. I'm going to charge in the room and announce I have committed this certain offense." He held up a hand to stay my question. "Don't worry, I didn't do it. Bram did. That will — let's say 'distract' — 'Mr. Moustache' in there, and then you sneak in, grab your sister, and go get your brother. I'll catch up as soon as I can."

"Got it."

With these words and a handshake, Oliver turned and ran down the hallway to the door of the room. He stared at me, pursing his lips, his legs poised to charge into the room. He took a deep breath, nodded with finality and threw the door open. He ran inside.

I shook my head. *Oliver's just got to make it.*

I ran to the same door and prepared to run in. I peeked in through the open door.

"Boris! No, I won't call you Mr. Carroph any longer. I have something to say to you," he announced to the astonished man. "I was the one who stole the turkey from the cellar last month." Boris' eyes narrowed and he inched closer to Oliver. Oliver continued. "And furthermore, I was the one who burned down the shed, *and* who let Latamer go." Oliver edged away as Boris came closer, his hands outstretched. "And... and..." Oliver continued, "I never liked you. You're a cruel, hard, ugly man. You're just a..." And he didn't even get to finish his sentence before Boris jumped him. The two fell to the ground, twisting and writhing in a wrestling mass of flesh.

I took my cue as everyone gasped to rush in. I ran around the table, grabbed the astounded Anne by the hand, yanked her out of her chair, flipped her on my back, and hightailed it out of the room.

I ran to the door, full of adrenaline. I didn't stop to consider someone might be guarding the door. But, alas, there was someone there. "Found ya, little darlins!" a voice cried. It was James. I couldn't get away before he had already grabbed hold of my arm. I slapped his hand to make him let go, but to no avail. Summoning strength I did not know I had, I tore my fingernails down his arm, leaving long streaks of blood.

He shrieked and let go of my arm. I ran down the long hallway to save mine and Anne's lives. My hair whipped my face as I pumped my legs back and forth.

I felt the same hand on my arm, much rougher. "Let me go!" I screamed.

"I don't think so, Missy," he said, his nostrils flaring. He clenched his jaw muscles and wrapped his hand around my throat. I gasped and choked, clawing at his hand. I felt Anne trying to help in some small way.

I managed to choke out just one word. "Indians!" I panted.

I must have hit a weak spot. The fire in his eyes died out and the blood in his face drained in an instant. He let go. "What are you talking about?" he demanded. I fell to the floor and took a sharp intake of breath, trying to regain my

composure. My throat felt like it was on fire. I wheezed,
spots flying before my eyes.

"What are you talking about?" he yelled.

"Fire," I gasped. "They... set fire... to the outside of...
the house," I said. I pointed to a corner of the house,
rasping.

The color drained from his face. He shouted "Kenneth!"

Kenneth soon appeared, looking very tired indeed. "Yes,
Mr. James, sir?"

"Take the girls and tie them up. I don't care where. Just
get them out of my sight. Then get outside! I need help!"

"Yes, sir." He led me by the arms past the corner where
I had been caught and then let me go. I sat Anne down,
trying to catch my breath. Looking into my eyes, he
whispered, "Alright, what's going on here?"

I was tired of giving phony explanations. We needed all
the help we could get. Besides, if I was wrong about his
loyalties, what was one more enemy?

"Oliver or Alexander, however you may know him and
my siblings and I are running away. Will you help us?"

He hesitated. "I... I can't. They'll hurt me if they catch
me." His face turned pink. He stared at his shoes, shifting
his weight from foot to foot. His face brightened. "Hey!
I've got it! I'll pretend I tied you two up but you escaped
behind my back! Okay?"

I nodded. "Perfect. Thank you." I tried to smile through
my racing nerves.

"Come sit in this room, in this chair. When you hear me
whistle twice, you can get up and leave, okay?" He clapped,
slow but delighted with his little plan.

I nodded again.

He lumbered outside. I sat in silence, awaiting the signal. My heartbeat drummed in my ears, every inch of my body pounding with adrenaline. Anne sat on the floor next to me, a bewildered but obedient toddler. I felt bad for her momentarily. She had no idea what was happening, poor thing. My mind flashed back to my purpose as I thought I heard a whistle. I searched the silence anxiously, making me imagine I heard sounds when I didn't. I rocked back and forth in my chair, growing antsy. Wait! Was that it? No, that was an animal. Was that —? No. It was someone else.

A-ha! At last I heard the whistle! I jumped up, swung Anne onto my back again, and ran out the door of the dark room.

Running back down the hallway, I saw Oliver bruised and unconscious. His rising and falling chest told me, although he was scratched up, he was alive. I saw no sign of Boris. I ran outside, watching for people guarding my way.

I emerged from the dangers of the cabin and smelled smoke. The Indians arrived at the same conclusion I did. In the far left corner of the house, a tongue of fire leaped out. *It's almost funny that after all that there was a fire.* James beat at the fire with his hat. Kenneth used his apron. Boris, who was bruised and limping heavily, toddled back and forth with buckets of water. Another man beat the flames with a rug. And none of them were making progress. I smiled. This would be the perfect distraction.

Anne and I ran past them. In all the chaos, they didn't notice us. I charged into the forest. The coolness of the shadows could comfort my nerves, but not today. I needed help, and quick.

About a half-mile into the forest, I tripped across a rock and fell, bringing Anne with me. My arm hit the rock on the way down and I felt blood start to trickle down my arm where it was cut.

My eyes teared up as I heaved to fill my lungs with air. I flopped onto the dirt, closed my eyes, and tried to shut out the nightmare surrounding me. I heard a noise. It sounded like a wagon. As the sound came closer, Anne stood and tried to pull me off of the road.

"Boo, come on," she urged.

My muscles twitched with exhaustion. Over the past week, I walked in the sun for twelve hours a day with little food and almost no water. I was beyond emotional exhaustion. I was worn to the edge of my limits. I was not about to move. "Help!" Anne shouted.

"Anne," I gasped. "You don't want the von Kruegers to hear us." She nodded and instead jumped up and down in the road, waving her arms.

With a squeal, the wagon stopped before me. I breathed a prayer of thanks I had not been run over after coming so far. The driver stepped down. "What's the matter, little one?"

I opened my eyes with a twinge of pain as Anne pointed to me. Not knowing how to explain what was wrong, she just said, "Boo's hurt."

"Ah," he whispered gently. With gentle arms, he picked me up and laid me in the seat next to him. "Miss, are you alright?" he asked in a deep and booming but kind voice. I watched as he took off his own scarf and tied it around my arm. The blood stained the pure white silk a muddy red. I nodded at him with silent gratefulness.

I saw a tall, well-dressed, clean-shaven man. He had straight black hair, large ears, and a square-cut jaw. I noticed he was tall; his lanky frame barely fit inside the carriage.

My lungs still heaving, I spoke between breaths. "Yes, but I need your help. Can you help me?"

He nodded. "Absolutely. What can I do?"

I stopped for a moment, appreciative he would take on such responsibility so readily.

"My brother was taken captive by the Indians and those men are after us." I gestured in their general direction, my breathing beginning to slow to normal. "We have to distract both groups in order to get my brother and my cousin away!"

He looked at me. "What's your plan?"

"Well, I... I guess I sort of figured... you would have a plan. After all, you're the adult."

He chuckled, urging the horse. "You're much closer to being an adult than you think. Age does not make maturity; remember that. Yah, Old Bob!"

I explained part of the plan to him as he brought us back to the house. As he tied his horse and cart to a tree, I assessed the situation.

The fire raged. It flickered over the roof and threatened to lick the overhanging tree branches of an old dead pine. More people fought the flames than when I left.

"Anne," I said, "I want you to stay here, right here, in this cart and we will be right back."

I realized I didn't know the man's name. "If you need me, or if someone's coming to get you, scream."

She nodded. Because I knew from experience Anne could scream louder than anyone I'd ever heard, I felt safe leaving her here for a moment. Trying to avoid all of the Kruegers, the man and I snuck back towards into the house. He had to duck as he entered the house. Oliver still lay unconscious in the entry room. The man swung him over his shoulder, coughing at the smoke filling the hall. I turned to run out. The smoke was too much for me; it brought back too many painful memories of home. I shuddered as the vision of Eli inside our burning home played yet again in my mind, as if it had been a week since the fire.

A thought occurred to me. Was there, in fact, someone still inside this place?

I ran past the room where the Indians had been, but it was empty. Then I found the room where we had all been seated. Annemarie remained in her chair unconscious. No one else remained. I did a quick mental count. That left eight children total, including the four with the Indians.

My dislike for Annemarie and my aversion to her strong, stubborn, rude ways were strong as I considered what to do. Should I risk myself to save her, or lose my conscience in saving myself? I could lose precious time if I tried to carry her myself.

My conscience won out. In a very unladylike manner, I slung her over my shoulder. I groaned at the extra weight.

Perhaps adrenaline had something to do with my unusual strength. She did not wake up as I staggered back to the man.

"Alright, I'm ready!" I yelled. I could barely hear over the crackle of the flames. My partner lumbered down the hallway, his tall frame causing him to scrape against the ceiling. We started to steal back to the wagon. Then I heard something: a piercing, painful shriek.

"CAARROOOLLLIIIINNNEEEE!" Anne screamed again.

I almost dropped Annemarie. I knew her fate alone and undefended would be no better than the sure death inside. I chose the sacrifice of saving her; now I would carry it through to the end. I ran as best I could, carrying her on my shoulder.

Regardless of my sarcastic burden, I was at the wagon within thirty seconds. I threw Annemarie in the wagon and turned to Anne; but she wasn't there.

"Anne?" I asked. But there was no answer. "Anne!" I shouted, turning in a circle. "ANNE!" I screamed.

She still didn't answer. Farther down the road, I saw where she had gone. The Indians took her. I groaned. My rescue mission increased; now I not only had to save Eli, Annemarie, Oliver, and myself, but also Anne.

My mind raced. I tried to propose a new plan but realized my original one was best. I had to alert the von Krueger's, the Indians were getting away. This would cause a distraction in the camp, and everyone could be rescued in the ensuing chaos. Anne's scream had already alerted them to the Indian's getaway, however; the von Kruegers were already mounting their horses to give chase.

The tall man led me back to the wagon. "Yah!" he shouted to his horse. He snapped the reigns and the horse took off. The cart rocked back and forth across the road, the limp and unconscious bodies of Oliver and Annemarie bumping against the sides of the wooden cart. I winced at the bruises they were sure to receive from it. We arrived at the edge of the Indian camp.

The encampment was filled with absolute disorder and confusion. Guns roared and knives flashed in the sun as man turned against man and brother against brother. It was an absolute massacre, and I had to make my way through it alive.

"For the souls of the warriors!" I heard one Indian cry as he charged into the chaos.

"For honor!" cried one of the men from the von Krueger's household.

"And revenge!" I heard James cry as he leapt into the bloodlust.

Indians ran in every direction, their faces blurred with those of the von Kruegers. I recognized some of the braves we had traveled with, along with some of the men I saw in the house. Dogs ran in circles, barking, and at the noise of the weapons, horses whinnied and flew up on their hind legs. Men ducked under these equine bridges, chasing the enemy. One man fell at the hands of the frenzied animals.

I set my eyes on the tent where I last saw Eli. I prayed Anne was in the same tent. I ran to it alone. My new friend's immense height would make him an easier target, so I had asked him to stay in the wagon.

I ducked under the flashing swords of men and pushed aside the hands of women who were setting fire to the surrounding fields in an attempt to wall in the enemy. I ran in between fist fights, leapt over the vicious dogs, and ran around the panicked horses. I knew I would do anything to get my siblings back in my arms. I heard someone groan and I felt the vibration of the ground as they fell. I jumped over the wounded soul to get into the teepee. With a gasp and a slight pause, I realized who it was. It was Kenneth, and he wasn't wounded—he was dead. My heart went out to the kind but simple boy who had saved us. He had sacrificed his long life for a people who didn't appreciate him. Running for my life, I reached the teepee.

Things were no better in there.

The cooking fire, now unattended, had sparked and started to spread on the corner of the animal-skin tent. All the children were huddled in the opposite corner, afraid of the fire but more afraid of the fate that awaited them should they attempt to go outside.

My face was dirty with soot, I smelled like smoke, and tears and sweat streaked down my face as I scanned the faces, my heart beating faster than I ever knew it could. Yet for all my sufferings my effort was worth it when I found him.

Eli gasped, jumped up, and hugged me. "Caroline!" he shouted. "I never thought I'd see you again." He buried his face in my dress.

My prayers were answered yet again; Anne, who was in the same teepee, soon joined our hug.

Eli drew himself up. "What's the plan?" he asked. I smiled at his bravery. "We don't have much of one except to keep everyone distracted while we run."

He squared his shoulders. "I see."

"There's not much time to waste, so…" I indicated the door flap of the tent with my head.

He shook his head. "I can't just leave everyone else here to die. We've got to take them."

"Eli…" I hesitated. "I'm afraid there isn't room. We can't. Come one, we've got to go!" I lunged towards the door.

He pulled my arm back. "We can at least try!"

"Elijah, there is no room!" I said with force, my voice raising to a panic. We were running out of time.

He came closer to me and leaned in towards me, whispering. "Caroline, there's always a way to do the right thing." He stood next to me, staring at me from under expectant eyebrows and awaiting the answer he knew I would give. Every child's frightened eye watched their fate unfold before them in my answer.

I sighed. "Alright, let's do it." Muffled cheers interrupted my next thought and I continued. "How are we going to get everyone out of here safely, though?"

A voice piped up from the corner. "Well, there's five of us," the child's voice offered.

"What does that have to do with anything?" I snorted.

"We could just run for it like you said, since there aren't that many of us!" another child suggested.

I shrugged. "Let's try it! On the count of three, everyone run, as fast as you can! If there's someone who can't walk, someone else carry him. Okay?"

They all nodded, preparing to run through the midst of the battle zone. I began counting. "One... two... three!"

With a sudden burst of energy, every child in the teepee shot outside. One little girl's legs were shooting back and forth, ducking and then jumping, her pigtails flying behind her. Another little boy grinned as he was being carried piggy-back style by his older sister. I carried Anne on my back.

"Over here, everyone!" I shouted.

They followed me like little ducklings follow their mother. Soon we emerged into the cool protection of the forest. Miraculously, no one saw us yet. The man jumped out of the wagon and helped me load the children into the back of the wagon in a frenzy. Oliver still lay unconscious inside, but Annemarie sat upright and cowered in the corner of the wagon. Her normal look of arrogance turned to a look of horror. I wanted to laugh at the poetic justice of the situation, if not for the urgency and her genuine fear. I took her limp, clammy, hand.

"Annemarie, it'll be alright. Don't worry." I smiled at her, and a little of the paleness in her face left. She flashed a weak smile.

I catapulted into the front seat of the wagon.

From behind us, I heard a loud yell, more a battle cry or a shout of alarm than anything else. A man armed with a rifle burst through the forest wall and shouted, "They're escaping!"

The voice seemed familiar, as did the face. I spent a nanosecond contemplating who he was before I recognized him. He was Dietrich von Krueger, the man who cornered us in Wichita Falls, the one taking such poor care of those orphans, the one who wore black and had a cane. I shivered as I put two and two together. Those were not orphans he had kept there. They were children kidnapped from their families and homes. That could have been—almost was—me.

The tall man took the reins of the horse and yelled, "Yah, Old Bob! Go!"

He snapped the reins. With a creak from the wagon, the horse ran. His sleek muscles rippled back and forth as in the background the others tried to muffle their cries of pain from the jolts. We didn't have much time to waste. The men were right on our trails. The path was straight and their horses were carrying less weight. They would catch up, unless my hero had a plan I didn't know about, and he did.

With a sharp turn, the man guided Old Bob around a corner I hadn't seen, nearly losing the wagon on the hard right. We plunged underneath a canopy of trees. The green leaves rushed past our wide and frightened eyes. Brown picket fences corralled us in on both sides. The logs were perhaps a foot from the side of the wagon. If I stuck my hand out of the wagon, the fence would have yanked it off. I wasn't sure we could fit through if the path got any thinner.

We had gained some time as the men did not expect
such a move. They were now about fifty feet behind us.
Their horses, carrying one man each, were far superior to
Old Bob, carrying a wagon load of people. As I had
predicted, they soon began to catch up.

The kind man leaned over to me. With a whisper, he
stated, "When I say 'go,' I want you and the other children
to jump to the left, over the fence. Run as fast as you can to
New Salem, and meet me in the 'First Berry-Lincoln
General Store.'"

I nodded and climbed in the backseat, notifying the
others of our dangerous and desperate plan. For what must
have been the hundredth time that day God in Heaven
heard our frightened prayers. Soon, the children were
awake, wide-eyed, and waiting for the signal to jump from a
moving wagon.

The more I yearned for the signal, the slower it seemed
to come. I was trapped in an eternity of waiting, of
nothingness, of the anxiety of wondering if I'd be ready
when the moment came. In that time span which felt like
an hour but lasted a few seconds, I heard the horses of the
men snorting and beating the ground behind me, the
anxious yells of our captors and the rumble of our wagon
on the bumpy road. My forehead broke out into a cold
sweat.

"Now!" our driver cried.

With one swift movement, we jumped over the wagon
side, over the fence, and landed roly-poly on the ground.
The procession of people thundered past us, the men

craning their necks to get one last angry glimpse of where we landed. I knew they would come back. We jumped up, readying to get on our way.

I counted the heads; good. Everyone made it. God heard my whispered prayer of thanks, again. One of the little boys whimpered as he sat on the ground. I leaned down to his level.

"Bayne, it will be alright," I soothed. I took his hand. His lip stuck out in a whimper.

"Thank you," his sister Eleanor mouthed at me. I nodded. "Now which way?" I said out loud. The man had told us to run, but he had not told us which way to run.

"Well... pick a direction, Caroline," offered Oliver.

"Yes, go ahead," cried Eleanor.

Anne patted me on the back. "You can do it, Boo," she said confidently.

I smiled. "I think one of us should climb a tree. Maybe we can see where the town is from there."

"I'll do it, Caroline!" Annemarie volunteered. Her hand shot up.

I gave her a quizzical look. "You?"

"Yes!" she bobbed her head.

"Ah... well...you may mess up your dress..." I said, sensing she was hardly ready to get down-and-dirty.

Her face grew a little pale. To her credit, however, she took a deep breath and replied. "Oh, fiddle-faddle. Who cares?" she said. She got a foothold on a tree, and with an adorable effort, tried to pull herself into the thin branches of a young pine, kicking and squirming.

Oliver lifted her down gently. "Try this one," he suggested, pointing to a sturdy oak.

She blushed and walked over to the tree. Oliver gave her a boost and she pulled herself into the tree, climbing higher and higher until she neared the top.

She spied in every direction and then climbed down, checking to make sure she placed her foot in the exact right spot every time. I looked behind us. We had a little bit of time, but how much I wasn't sure.

I heard everyone gasp. My gaze shot up to Annemarie. She swayed on one of the highest branches, wobbling and lurching around in the thin, cold air. Then, with a death-grip, she leaned forward and clutched the knotty old tree like it was her only hope of survival, which of course it was. I don't believe a one of us took a single breath until she touched the ground, very pale-faced indeed.

"Well?" I asked, breathing again.

She pointed to the North. "There's a town right over there," she said weakly.

Squaring our shoulders, we marched North for the next half-hour. We came upon the edge of an adorable town.

On our right and left were small log cabins, their stone chimneys blackened with many a past winter's fires. Little flowers were growing in front of the houses, and little boys and girls played on the streets, laughing and chattering. In front of us lay a blacksmith's shop. We walked past it and heard the heavy clanging of the cooper pounding out the metal and smelled the hot, metallic smell of molten iron. A small courthouse sat in the center of the village, and far to our right was a water-wheel. It was swishing with a rhythm of the sounds of the village. And, only a few houses in front of us, sat the Lincoln-Berry General store, flanked by an old, sweaty horse in the pasture next to it. I smiled. The man had made it back.

We plunged into the front door as the bell chimed, making known our entrance. The tall man noticed us from behind the counter and smiled.

"Welcome, children! I'm so glad you made it. I was worried about you."

I shook his hand, beaming. "Sir, thank you so much for everything! I can't imagine what we would have done without you."

He interrupted. "Oh, really now, I'm not as great as all that. I am delighted to help anyone who needs it." He smiled a broad, friendly smile grew as it spread across the faces of all of us in the room. He continued. "Well! Your captors are gone and I remain victorious."

I interrupted. "They didn't hurt you when they caught up, did they? I'd feel horrible if you were injured on our accounts!"

"Actually, they didn't catch me. Since you children were gone, the men had no reason to chase me any longer."

"Oh," I replied.

After a short silence, he asked, "So, what is your plan now, children?"

We examined ourselves and knew we needed a plan now.

"Well, sir, Bayne and I want to go back home to Ma and Pa. They're prob'ly real worried about us," Eleanor offered.

"Yup," Bayne agreed.

"My Ma is gone and my Pa was killed in the war," said Annemarie. "I've got no place to go back to." She shuffled around awkwardly.

"And neither have I," said Oliver.

"Me too," said Terry, a quiet little girl with pigtails.

The man nodded. "I see." He turned to Annemarie and kept speaking.

I didn't hear what was said as I walked over to Eli and whispered to him instead.

Eli's eyes brightened and he nodded. He whispered back in my ear. I nodded as well. I pulled Oliver to the side and whispered in his inclined ear. "Oliver," I said, "Eli and I just talked about it, and we were wondering... we're going to our Great-grandmother's house in Ohio. We started with six people and now we have three. We could always use another pair of hands. Do you want to come with us?" He pulled away in surprise and stared at me, smiling. I pulled him back closer to finish my question. "The only thing I ask is I be in charge. I'm the one who started this journey, and I need to be the one to finish it."

He looked confused and leaned over to ask me a question when our tall helper joined us and spoke. "Well, let me be the first to tell you the city of New Salem will be more than glad to harbor children as long as they need it. Now, children, you may go out and play if you'd like. When you get hungry, just ask for Mary Todd."

Annemarie, Eleanor, Bayne, and Terry laughed and left to play.

"Wait!" he called.

They all turned back around. He reached under the counter and brought out some licorice sticks.

"Here you are," he said. He placed them over the counter into the glad hands of the children.

They grinned and ran outside to play, laughing. Eli, Oliver, Anne and I remained.

He turned to Oliver. "Now as for you, young man..." He leaned back as he stroked his stubble-free chin. "You look like the prime age to become an apprentice."

Oliver shrugged. "I'm not sure yet what I want to do. Other people have always told me what to do... Now I'm free, I guess I don't *have* a plan."

The tall man stroked his chin as he looked at the ceiling, a mere seven inches from the top of his head. "Do you suppose you would be willing to come help me? I've been looking for someone to teach my law practice to. Perhaps someday you could even take over." He winked at our cousin.

Oliver's face brightened. "Now that's an idea," he mused. He looked down at his own hand and then thrust it out. Our tall friend shook it. "It's a deal," Oliver said.

The contagious laughter of Oliver's new teacher sounded. "Now would be a proper time to ask your name," he said.

Oliver chuckled. "After you, sir!"

"I am Abraham Lincoln, esquire. But most people just call me Abe." He winked. "And yours?"

"My name is Alexander, sir." I elbowed him and he took the hint. "I'm sorry; I've been used to being called

Alexander. My real name is Oliver. Oliver Wendell Holmes."

They shook hands again. "Pleased to meet your acquaintance, Mr. Holmes. It will be my privilege to teach you all I know of the law." Mr. Lincoln smiled.

Eli and I stood in place, hands behind our backs quietly. We looked at each other with strained smiles. Oliver seemed to remember we were there too. He smacked his forehead.

"Where are my manners? This is my cousin, Caroline Darley, her brother, Elijah, and her sister, Anne."

"Good to meet you," he said, smiling. We each shook his hand and returned the smile.

"May I give you each a little something?" he asked. "You could use a treat." He chuckled.

"Thank you," I replied politely.

Our tall friend reached behind him and spoke as he moved. "Now this is for you, young man," he said to Eli. Eli rocked on the balls of his feet, grinning in expectation. Mr. Lincoln brought out a well-worn book. "This used to be mine when I was young," he said. "I think you'll find it enjoyable."

Eli gasped and took hold of the book. "For me?" he asked, glancing into Mr. Lincoln's eyes. "For you," he replied with a deep voice.

"Thank you," Eli breathed. He went out of the front door, his nose already buried in the book.

"You seem like you are in dire need of a doll, little one," he directed to Anne.

"A dolly?" Anne cried.

He smiled. "How's this?" Mr. Lincoln asked. He brought from under the counter a beautiful little doll with a simple cotton dress and yarn hair. It couldn't have been more perfect for the happy little girl. She squealed and ran outside, clutching it to her chest. Mr. Lincoln laughed as he turned to me.

"And for you?" he asked, winking.

I had a perfect idea. "Do you happen to know what a Hydra plant is?"

He nodded. "I know them very well," he said. "Here they're called Long-arms. Why?"

"Do… do you happen to have one?" I asked doubtfully.

He walked over to the windowsill and grabbed a plant potted in a small clay container. It had a long, dark green stem and the leaves were arranged in an odd circular fashion, so that it appeared to have several arms. He brought it over to me and set it on the counter.

"Is this…" I breathed, touching its leaves.

"Yes, it's the plant you need. It's a Hydra plant. It's for you." He pushed it towards me and smiled.

"But… I don't know how to take care of it or anything," I objected.

"There are a handful of things you need to know. First, the flower lasts three weeks, and secondly, this flower has been alive for about two days."

I interrupted, studying the plant. "Oh, that's no problem! The bulb is what I need. It will last much longer, long enough to get me there."

"This plant is different," he continued. "After the flower dies, so does the bulb." He reflected a moment then corrected himself. "Actually, it's not quite immediate. Once the flower wilts away and drops all but two of its petals, then the bulb shrivels up and dies. I would say within three days of that." My head spun with all of the information I knew I would never remember. "The total life of the plant is just over three weeks—twenty-two days in total. You may be able to use it one day after that, or perhaps it will be too late. It's impossible to tell."

I turned to him. "What you're telling me is I have twenty-three days, including today and the possibility of the extra day after the flower dies, to get to Ohio, or else this will be unusable and my Great-grandmother will die."

He nodded. "Yes."

A-ha. That's why no one imported it — they wouldn't have enough time to get to New Salem, get the flower, and come back before it died. I found my answer to the question I had asked John, and it wasn't good news by a long shot.

I took a deep breath. "I suppose I'd better get going, then."

He leaned over the counter and shook my hand. "May God speed your journey, Miss," he said.

"Thank you," I said. I squeezed his hand. I turned to walk out of the door, but then remembered something. "By the by, I think you should wear a beard. You would look a great deal better. Your face is quite thin!"

He stroked his chin. "A beard, eh? I'll consider it." He smiled.

I smiled back at him, nodding. I walked out the door and heard it ding. I motioned to Eli and Anne, who were sitting on the steps and entertaining themselves with daisy chains. "Come on, siblings," I said. "We've got a long way to go."

Little did I know there was something lurking in the woods, its eyes following our every move.

The Same Fate

WE WALKED THROUGH the Indiana prairie two weeks later. I tracked our progress.

We left New Salem two weeks ago, leaving Oliver in the good, strong hands of Mr. Lincoln. We traveled thirty miles in two days, and the day after about twelve. Then, in the next week or so, we made it almost 120 miles, and the two days after bore a prize of thirty-five miles. Today, I estimated we went about fourteen. The numbers spun in my head, telling me an average of three miles an hour was not enough.

Eli, Anne and I were hungry, thirsty, tired, and much more tanned than we were when we left Mr. Lincoln. Every day when we woke to the rising sun, our schedule was to grab a quick breakfast if possible, and then go. For about three miles we ran, then rested for half an hour, then jogged before giving in to walking.

I tried to estimate the mileage in my head. I turned to Eli after a moment of trying in vain. "Eli, how much is thirty plus twelve plus one hundred and twenty plus thirty-five plus fourteen?"

He pinched the bridge of his nose and scrunched his eyes closed. "Two hundred and eleven."

I grinned. Not every nine-year old can add five numbers without a slate board or a piece of chalk!

I tried to focus on how to improve our speed as I walked. It was better than thinking about my intense thirst. We didn't pass a stream, creek, or river for two days. My forehead sweltered with the heat — I didn't have enough water in my body to make sweat. I swallowed what I could muster, my throat burning, and concentrated on my math and geography to forget the thirst. My tongue felt thick and fuzzy. I shook my head, dismissing the thoughts of my thirst.

Assuming Eli was right, there were one hundred and fifty miles left in our trek, with seven days left to walk it. I smiled. Seeing how well we did in the past week, it seemed possible we would make it.

A cold wind gusted through the forest and I shivered. It was October 12th now. Winter trailed us. I sighed and walked faster.

I heard Eli grunt in the background. I turned.

"Eli, are you okay?"

"Yes, I'm fine," he murmured from the ground. I helped him to his feet.

He took a few steps then fell again, twisting his ankle in an unnatural position. "Eli!" I leaned down to help him to his feet again.

"I'm fine, I'm fine," he said. He waved me off.

"Let me see your ankle," I said.

I lifted the pant leg a little off of his ankle and gasped. It was red and swollen. "Eli, this is swelling. Why did you tell me you were fine?"

"What? It is?" He peered down at his ankle.

"Ye-esss," I answered slowly. "Do you not feel it?"

He shook his head. "Not at all. It's numb. Has been for a while," he said. He blew warmth into his hands.

I felt a sudden chill come through me. Winter was closer than I thought. "Alright, here. Get onto my back," I said. I lifted him onto my back and turned to continue.

Something caught my eye. There were horse prints on the ground. The gears of my mind began to turn. Since there were no people around, the horses wouldn't be owned, and that meant... I smiled again as I formulated a plan. It was getting cold, and we needed a faster mode of transportation. Horses would do just fine.

"Eli, do you think you could you come help me? Don't overexert yourself, though," I added.

He shrugged and walked over. "Doesn't hurt me right now, anyway," he said.

I tugged at a dark green vine on top of one of the branches.

Eli hesitated. "But... ah, Caroline...? What are you doing?"

I grunted as I yanked on the very tight wound plant. "I need to make a lasso."

"A lasso? Why do we need a lasso?"

I turned and put my hands on my hips. "To rope something with, of course." I rolled my eyes and turned back. I *tsk*-ed. "Why do we need a lasso…" I muttered. As my fingers wrapped around the cold, hard, almost muscular vine, I noticed the texture was peculiar. I shrugged. Eli stood behind me and bit his lip. He joined me after a moment.

He tugged. "Caroline, are you feeling alright?"

"Oh, I'm fine. Just help me," I snapped.

"Are you sure? You look a little tired."

"Of course I'm tired. I'm also thirsty, and a little hungry. Are you going to call the Nutrition Deputy or can we get on with this?"

He shook his head. "Alright, if you say so." He stood beside me and used his weight to tug on a different vine. I yanked on the branch. It didn't give at all.

I heard Eli scream. "Caroline, look out!" He screamed. I looked up.

My hands were wrapped around a cottonmouth — and it was angry.

I screamed and fumbled with it.

It opened its mouth wide as I stumbled backwards out of the water, yelling.

The snake came closer, its teeth glistening. It hissed, spitting and baring its fangs. I was close enough to see the white in its mouth for which it was named.

It darted out.

"Boo!" Anne screamed.

My last thought before everything went black was falling into the water. I wish I drank some of the water before I died.

I awoke to find myself not quite as dead as I originally believed. That is to say, not dead, but feeling as if I were.

The immediate scan of my surroundings told me I was in a pitch-black room with a wet sponge on my face. I tried to twist away.

"There, there, honey," said a smooth voice. Gentle hands massaged my arm as I blinked back into full consciousness.

I tried to sit up. "Wh-where am I?" I asked, rubbing my eyes. I tried to concentrate through the haze.

"You're with Auntie Vivian, dear." She lowered me back onto my pillows, clearing my hair from my face.

"Where are my siblings?"

Her quiet voice was muffled in the dark room. "I don't think you should know until you're quite well again." She patted my head with the wet cloth again.

A pang went through my heart. I sat up, getting the sheets caught on the sequins of my outfit. "Tell me!"

"I will, in time," she said.

"Tell me now!" I pounded my fist on the mattress and sat up. Black spots swam before my eyes. I forced down the rising vomit. I found myself sinking back onto the pillows.

She let out a lingering sigh. "Alright, I'll tell you," she said with a quivering voice. She laid a hand on my arm. The need for pity in whatever she was going to tell me sent fire through my heart. "You... you stopped off the road for a moment. And the branch you tugged on was not a branch, it was a cottonmouth."

"I know that. Move on! Where are my siblings," I pressed?

"Have patience, dear," she answered. "I'm getting there. The cottonmouth bit you, but after you passed out it didn't let go of you—it just held on. Your brother dragged you off the road." She let out another trembling sigh. "When he turned to go get your sister, he met the snake's mate." I let out a tiny gasp—all my beating heart could stand. She kept her next words short. "It bit him on the ankle, he fell into the water, and he... he drowned, dear." Her voice quivered. I let out another tiny squeak.

My head shook back and forth. "No, no, no." I squeezed my eyes closed. "I don't believe it! This must be a dream. It can't be true!"

I pinched myself, again and again.

I did not wake. "No!" I screamed in frustration. I tried to slap myself. She caught my weak hand. "Let me go!"

"Child, I know this is hard to accept, but you have to face it. Your brother is dead, dear," she said.

"Take me to him!" I shouted.

"I buried him," she replied to my hysterics.

"Then... take me to his grave." I whispered. The words tasted vile in my mouth. I just knew it couldn't be true. He couldn't be dead. No, no, no. I needed him. No. Not Eli.

Not my baby brother. Not him. It couldn't be true. I could almost hear him calling!

She sighed again. "Alright, child." She put her arm beneath my head, picked me up, and carried me to the gravesite, for I was not yet strong enough to walk.

We plunged into the misty outside. My stomach was rolling too violently to listen, but as we walked I heard her soothing voice continue to speak in the background. I tried to tune in for some pieces of her information.

"I buried him myself, honey," she said quietly. "I would know." She continued after a moment. "Your sister is the one who found me," she said. "She's a very wonderful little girl... A very wonderful little girl," she repeated.

I turned my head away, trying to make it clear I was not going to respond anytime soon.

Then we got to Eli's grave. My eyes could not stop running over the simple words. "Here lies a boy, drowned. 1856." It seemed to me I saw the faint outline of a boy, standing beside it, reaching for me with downcast eyes.

The words pulsated in my mind, growing and shrinking and growing and shrinking and spinning — I screamed and closed my eyes, shutting out the horrible sight.

Pinching yourself in a dream does not work, because I screamed again and awoke.

"Caroline! Are you alright?" cried Eli. He sat on his knees, fanning me.

I found myself breathing hard. "Eli!! You're alive!"

He looked at me askance. "Yes, I am. Why do you say that?"

I opened my mouth to explain but shook my head. "Never mind. There's too much. Where am I? What happened?" I found myself covered with mud and sitting in a ditch.

"We're in the forest, Boo!" Anne said, squatting beside me.

Eli answered the other part of my question. "When you and I pulled on the vine, the branch it was wrapped around fell down and hit you on the head," he said. "You've still got quite a bump." He reached up and brushed his fingers across a spot on the back of my head.

I jumped and batted his hand away. "No kidding," I agreed. "So the vine wasn't a snake?"

"No..." he replied, furrowing his eyebrows.

"Then... then I suppose you have never heard of Auntie Vivian?"

"Andy Viv-yen?" Anne said.

Eli shook his head in assent. I beamed and hugged them both.

A tear danced on the edge of my eyelashes. "It was all a dream, Eli," I said, my face close to his.

"What was a dream, Caroline?" he asked patiently. I hugged him again, then held him at arm's length, staring him in the eyes. "Wait. What day is it?? We haven't lost time, have we?"

"It's still Sunday, Caroline. You've been out ten minutes," he replied, worried at my odd behavior. "Caroline, are you sure you're alright? You don't look so good. Go look at yourself in the creek."

Ah-ha! So that's why they looked so refreshed — they found water! I limped, my head aching, over to where Eli led me as I leaned on his thin frame. I pulled back to keep myself from sticking my entire head in the water. I slurped and slurped, not stopping until I coughed from drinking too quickly. I viewed my reflection in the rippling water. My beautiful brown hair looked like a rat's nest of frizzy tangles. A knob the size of a goose egg throbbed on my head. My normal clear complexion was bright red and freckled. No wonder Eli asked if I felt alright.

My smile faded and the normal sparkle in my eyes died with the desperation of our situation. My hallucination, the dryness of my tongue, our empty stomachs and my brother's death convinced me.

I sunk to the ground. Another drop of water rolled off my face and joined the ones rippling in the pond.

There's nothing you can do about it. Fix your hair and let's get going — this isn't a lost cause yet.

"It's no use," I retorted to myself. "I just can't do it."

I felt myself losing the will to move. I started to fall back to the ground. *You're so close!*

"Yes, but what could happen in those last hundred and fifty miles? And besides, what about that hallucination?" I whispered back. "What if it meant something more?"

It's not what could happen as much as what will happen. If you don't get going, then you, Eli and Anne will all die, and no one will know.

"Yes, because we're in the middle of nowhere with no help and no adults, I moaned".

My thoughts interrupted my complaint. "Furthermore, you won't be fulfilling your parent's last wishes, and your Great-grandmother will die."

But! if you get up and persevere in love and faith, you may just make it!

I sighed and stirred to my knees. Looking better was the first step to feeling better. I dipped my head into the cool, clear water. Lifting it up, dripping, I flung back my head and shook out my hair. I checked my reflection in the rippling water. It looked much better. I splashed water over my face, taking a deep breath.

Perhaps we could make it, even if winter was coming soon. But to do that, we'd have to hurry. I motioned to my siblings and we hit the road again.

I couldn't come up with a counter-argument for the vision meaning more than just a dream. My wide gaze shot to Eli. He walked alongside me, playing with the flowers in his path. He laughed and jumped as he disturbed the quiet patch of daisies which sat in the path, playing like a normal little boy should.

I couldn't lose Eli. I needed him to help me with the small remnant of my broken family, the only one of us able to help and support me. *That dream must not come true.* I reached out to him and hugged him again. I tousled his mop of blonde curls and he smiled.

To quote from Mr. Scrooge, I thought, 'They are here – I am here — the shadows of the things would have been, may be dispelled. They will be. I know they will.'

A cold and rainy night did not boost our morale. I shivered as I searched for a good place to camp. I trotted ahead, searching for a warm place to rest for a moment, perhaps a dry tree or a thick grassy knoll. But as I rounded the corner I found something better. A nice little cave to sleep in! It was dry, would keep in heat, and was hidden enough most large animals either wouldn't find it or wouldn't fit in the small entrance. It was perfect.

"Eli! Anne!" I called.

They soon appeared. I pointed to the cave, smiling. They grinned, relaxing at the prospect of a warm place to sleep. Eli picked up a branch and busied himself by breaking it into smaller fire wood. I picked up larger branches and snapped them into larger pieces than Eli ended up with—fuel would last longer. I ducked inside the cave and, with a branch of green leaves, cleared out the dead leaves and dust collected there.

As soon as we had the fire wood ready, complete with the twigs, dry leaves, and other flammable things on bottom, I began to rub two sticks together (a trick I had learned on this trip). Soon we had a nice cozy fire going. A warm and pleasant light furthered our sleepiness. It popped and crackled as the air bubbles inside the wood were exposed to the heat. Above us a noisy wind groaned, throwing around the arms of the trees right outside the cave and causing thick grey clouds to sweep past the full moon.

Too exhausted to wish each other pleasant dreams, we all three collapsed on the floor of the cave.

The coolness of the night kept me awake. I did some calculations in my head. If it was this cold already, then in two more weeks it would be twenty degrees cooler. By then, there was a danger we could freeze, not having coats, mittens, or blankets at our disposal. My mind wandered to places where it was dangerous for me to explore. I saw the picture of Eli and Anne and me lying on the ground, blue, frozen, and never to move again. I saw Great-Grandmother Pamela wondering why no one would bring her the flower, not knowing three children had tried... and died. I shivered and tried to cast off the gruesome images.

I craved the comfort Eli provided when we were with the Indians. I rotated towards him. "Eli!"

He did not answer.

I shook him. "Eli!" I said.

He did not wake.

I became frightened. I saw every piece of my vision coming back to haunt me. I threw him back and forth. "Eli!"

His eyelids came open. "What, Caroline? I was sleeping!"

I let out a deep sigh of relief, tears of simultaneous fright and relief squeezing out of my eyes. I turned my head, ashamed lest he see my fear over nothing.

"Nothing," I replied. "Go back to sleep."

Very grateful, he turned back over and closed his purple eyelids. And just like that, I was alone again in a world felt hostile to me. I was afraid and helpless in a strange place.

"Six days left."

I noticed my peaceful siblings, wishing I could do something to keep them innocent and sweet forever. *See, everything is fine. No need for worry.* I hesitated for a moment. *Everything will be fine, right?* I nodded. "Yes. Fine."

We went foraging for some breakfast, whatever it may end up being. As was our custom, Eli and Anne went one way and I went the other, being careful not to stray too far from one another. I rounded the corner to find a dense cluster of mushrooms! *What luck is mine!* I picked them and placed them into my skirt. I used to go mushroom-hunting with Papa, and we picked these all the time. I knew they were safe. After I had picked all the safe mushrooms, I traipsed back to the camp.

I came back to find yet another surprise — Eli and Anne, both holding dressfuls, or shirtfuls in Eli's case, of cranberries! We gorged ourselves on our first feast in what seemed like forever. By the time we finished, all our mouths were stained red from the cranberries and our tongues spicy from the mushrooms.

We stood and went on our way.

I heard a noise in the bush. It sounded loud over the pounding of my heart.

A bunny emerged from the bush, twitched its nose, and scampered away. I let out my breath.

Nothing happened all day; in fact, the most exciting event of the day was when Eli tripped and cut his arm on a bramble bush. We cleaned it and were on our way again.

We stopped for the night. I sat under a small rock overhang, shaking my head in disbelief as I gave thanks for the non-events of the day. We had gone seventeen miles; a long distance for three tired children. We then found a big apple tree in the middle of the day. Two feasts in one day, and nothing had gone amiss.

So what's the catch? I wondered. *Is it actually possible for me to do no more than have a good day?*

"I believe I just did," I said out loud.

"What?" said Eli.

"I said, 'I believe I just did.'" I smiled and corralled Anne into my arms, stroking her hair.

She smiled, cuddled up to me, and after a moment went to sleep.

And, satisfied with a good day, so did I.

I sighed at the wilting Hydra.

"We've got the rest of today and tomorrow to get the remaining twenty-seven miles," I said to Eli. I sighed and turned back to survey the land. My lips pursed as the wind blew strands of my hair in my face.

"Well," he said, "Papa said she lived *near* Springfield, Ohio, not *in* it. So maybe she's only ten or so miles away." He gestured with his hands as he spoke.

"Still," I replied, "Perhaps she's not on the close side of town. As it is, we'd have to go nine more miles today and eighteen tomorrow." I looked up at the grey, cloudy sky. "We need to get a move on," I said.

"I'm trying, Boo, but my feet hurt. You walk a lot faster than me," said Anne, joined the conversation.

I softened, remembering her tender age of four. I leaned down to her level and took her hand. "I'm sorry, Anne. If your feet start to hurt, tell me and I'll help you." I turned to look at my brother. "Eli, that goes for you, too."

They both nodded as I stood. We quickened our pace. Thunder rumbled in the distance, and if I had examined the Hydra, I would have seen one of the four leaves left fall off of the it in the frosty wind.

Eli stopped behind us and bent to the ground. "Hey Caroline," Eli said, "Look at this."

"Yes?"

He pointed to something on the ground.

"Be careful…" I warned, approaching him sideways.

"Don't worry," he answered.

I edged closer and peered at the thing to which he was pointing.

It was a large paw print, about five inches in diameter. The huge animal would be powerful. The fresh-looking print was pressed deep into the mud. The two-inch claw marks helped me to identify it as the one thing I hoped not to see since Mama and Papa's passing: the mark of a panther.

My eyes grew wide.

"Don't worry, Caroline," Eli said, "it's about three days old. However," he shuddered, glancing around at the tall grasses, "I would feel much safer if we got out of here."

"I agree," I responded.

I put Anne on my back for maximum speed and we left. We exited the field and came upon a cleared section. About five hundred feet away sat a little glade. We stumbled towards it, exhausted by our impromptu run.

Thunder rumbled in the distance again. I smelled the metallic scent of rain on the heavy wind. It blew up my dress as the gusts increased. The first pattering drops of a thick storm began falling, but soon it was heavy. Anne was blinking to keep the sharp rain out of her eyelashes, and Eli's curls were plastered to his face. He pushed them out of his eyes and kept moving.

Soon there was a rush of swishing sounds as the shower turned into a storm. Lightning flashed, the subsequent thunder booming like a drum in my ears and echoing. I could not see through the thick wall of pouring water. I joined Anne in blinking, trying to keep the water out of my eyes.

"Caroline!" Eli called from somewhere behind me. His voice was muted by the pattering sounds of the raindrops on the grass.

I turned around, looking for him. I could not see him through the water, which meant he could not see me, either.

"We're here, Leli!" Anne shouted. I would have smiled at the way her toddler tongue pronounced 'Eli' when she was upset, except for the rapid rising storm which took precedence in my mind. "I can't see you!" He sounded panicked.

"Just follow my voice," I coached, trying to sound soothed in my shouting.

Just then, lightning struck a tree about thirty feet ahead
of me, causing an explosion of light and sparks jumping
from the tree. I stumbled backwards and landed on my rear
end in the mud, dropping Anne. "Are you alright?" he
shouted.

"Yes, just a little startled," I cried. I turned to Anne and
lifted her. I reached to brush off her dirty dress but
because of the mud on my hands I left a streak of dirt
instead. "Oh, Anne, I'm sorry…"

"S'okay, Boo," she replied. She clambered up my back
and didn't worry about the dress. It would be washed out in
the rain anyway.

Eli found me and took my arm. "I'll bet you were
startled. That one was — pretty"

I could not hear the rest of what he said for the thunder.
It drummed in our ears, vibrating our ribs and seeming to
crush our eardrums. I squinted, wincing. The wind drove
the biting rain into my nearly-bare arms. I shivered and
wrapped my arms around the thread-bare dress which
Rachel had gifted me so long ago.

"It's dangerous for us to be out here, Caroline," Eli
yelled. "We'd better find some shelter."

I nodded and we stumbled over to the nearby forest. The
rain was lighter here. I guessed the high and intertwining
branches blocked off much of it. We sat down next to a
hollow "Grandmother Tree" and I let Anne slide off my
back. We rested against the bark gratefully. My red feet
were swollen and swore, and I rubbed them as Eli yanked a

branch off a tree. He snapped it in half to make a walking stick.

Glancing over at Eli, I said, "Eli, don't do that to the tree. Mama always said it hurts it."

Anne, not one to sit still for long, was soon up and about, exploring the little glade we had found.

"Anne, wait," Eli called, "don't go off by yourself. Let me walk with you." He groaned as he put his tired and swollen joints back into use, but he went nonetheless.

I steeled myself to go join them after a moment of resting and watching them.

Anne limped over to a pond created by the storm and Eli came behind her, slipping and sliding on the mud.

I closed my eyes for a moment, folded my hands on my stomach, and took a deep breath. I was not going to nap, but perhaps rest for a moment.

Then there came a high-pitched, very loud scream, a more masculine, but no less terrified, one, and two thuds. My stomach rolled as my eyelids snapped open, petrified to see what had happened but petrified not to.

Both Anne and Eli were gone. They were gone—no trace of them.

My mouth dropped open and I shot to my aching feet. I was otherwise paralyzed with shock. My siblings were gone, and all I had left of them were a scream and the walking stick Eli had dropped. What had happened?

Then, a long second later, a timid voice asked, "Caroline?"

I let out a sigh of relief as I wiped my clammy hands on the side of my skirt. "Eli? Anne? Where are you?"

"Down here!" Anne's muffled voice yelled.

I approached the spot where they were when last I saw them. I leaned a little farther, trying to see them — then whump! I fell into the same hole they had and landed on my rear end. I didn't know I fell until I was down. My hand searched for the Hydra before it was lost; it was Great's only hope and mine too. I wasn't about to lose it. I leaned back and stared up through the thirty-foot, dripping, muddy hole I had fallen into. It was a slick climb with nothing to hold onto all the way up, and it even looked like there may have been another level above us before the surface. I could not even reach the top of the first even halfway-decent holding point.

I turned over to Eli. "What happened?"

His eyes squeezed shut as he rocked back and forth, cradling his swelling ankle. It was beginning to bruise already. "I think it's sprained," he moaned.

"Let me see." I knelt down and examined the ankle.

I brushed my fingers over it. He yelled at the pain and I jumped.

"It's definitely sprained," I confirmed.

"So what do we do to fix it?" he said, wincing.

I looked around for some means of wrapping it up.

I had an idea. I had done this once, so I may as well do it again. I put my back to Eli and tore off a piece of my underskirt for a splint.

As I pulled it away, something fell to the floor, pieces of a leaf and the edge of a piece of string. *Now why would I have leaves and string in my skirt?* I wondered. I thought back, trying to remember why I might have put those in my pocket. Then it came in a flash — those were Henry's anti-aching leaves! I gasped. I forgot I put them in my skirt. Now we could eat them! I looked to either side of me, wishing I had water to make tea with the crunched-up bits. I saw none. Eating them straight would have to do instead.

I bent and sorted through the many sticks had fallen to the floor over the years and selected a good-sized one for a splint. I crawled over to Eli and eyed him. "Eli, this is going to hurt, but the leaves should help." He nodded.

With my heart throbbing to every whimper escaping his lips, I wrapped the makeshift splint around Eli's ankle, keeping it steady. His lip bled from biting it in an attempt to keep in his cries. "Alright. Now keep it elevated." I sighed and turned to the dark tunnels, my hands on my hips. "Okay. I'm going to explore this tunnel; you two stay here. Yell if you need help." I turned to go.

"No!" Eli cried, startling me and making me turn around. "Please, don't leave us alone. You said you'd carry me if I needed help... Well, now I need help." His face streaked with dirt, sweat, and I'm sure not a few tears.

I wavered in between carrying him and leaving them. I couldn't decide if coming or staying was safer.

"Boo..." Anne breathed. She toddled over to me and grabbed my leg. I looked down as I felt her tears caress my leg. "You look just like Mama," she said. I looked up and Eli nodded, his eyes closed with approval.

I realized she was right. This was like Mama, right before she had died. When she was deciding between going to help Papa and leaving us alone.

This likeness caused me to decide. I leaned down and picked up Eli, ignoring the throbbing complaints in my feet. He held on to my neck as I plunged into the unknown. Anne clung to my leg, keeping her fear locked inside. I looked around in the silence, trying to find some way out. Only the faint sound of a drop falling into a pool echoed somewhere in the distance.

"Which way?" I wondered aloud.

Eli pointed to one of the tunnels. "If I'm right, that way should lead closer to Great," he said.

I shook my head with determination. "May as well," I said.

After about five minutes, I had managed to lead us down a long tunnel with no light. I could no longer see the way to get out and it led nowhere. Just as I started to panic, Eli broke the silence. "Boy, it sure is dark, huh?" He let out a nervous laugh.

"Yeah, and cold," I answered trying to keep the tiny bud of morale alive.

Our voices echoed in the quiet. I still heard the faint drip-drip through the still caverns. I shuddered as I peered into the nothingness and wondered where it led, and what was concealed in it.

I spoke louder than necessary to create some sound, so it wouldn't be so quiet. "Eli, Anne, I think it's time to go back. We'll figure this out in the morning, when maybe we can see better. For all I know, it's dark because the sun has already set."

I saw the faint outline of Eli moving next to me. "No, wait! I think I see some light ahead," he said.

"Where?" I peered into the darkness.

He pointed into the distance. "Don't you see it? It's right there. I feel like I could almost touch it."

"Eli, I think maybe you're just wanting to see it," I soothed.

"No, really! I see... I think... yes, I see some plants there and everything!"

I gave him a doubtful look, though he couldn't see it for the enveloping blackness. "Caroline, just trust me! Have I ever been wrong before?"

"Yes," Anne volunteered.

"Well, this time I'm not!" he retorted.

I sighed and walked to the place he directed. To my great surprise and enjoyment, we did indeed come upon a small sliver of light, complete with a green plant blooming underneath its tender care. As I went around the plant, trying to discern whether or not it was edible, I found myself stepping into the muddy stream.

"Water," I announced. No one made a move—not yet. With Anne's cholera we had all learned to be cautious of dirty water when we had any choice to be.

"Caroline, I'm hungry. Do you think we could eat that fruit? I've never seen it before."

"Eh... I don't know. I don't recognize it, so we'd better not. At least until we're really starving." I gave him a look. "It's been a couple hours since we ate." I didn't realize how tired I was until my knees started to buckle under me. "Let's take a break," I announced.

We plumped down on uphill slant and didn't talk. I tried not to stare at the alluring tree as my mouth grew drier all the time. My tongue felt thick and fuzzy, my lips seeming more and more cracked every second. I forced myself to look away. Feeding my hunger pangs was not worth the danger of eating the unknown fruit.

After about ten minutes, however, I couldn't resist any longer. I jumped up, picked a piece of the thick pink fruit, and threw another piece to Eli and another to Anne.

Eli set the fruit down on the ground. "Caroline, are you sure? You *said* —"

But I was already digging in. The taste was delicious, better almost than anything I had ever had. The sweet and tingling juices ran down my throat and across my fingers.

As I chewed and swallowed the odd textured fruit, my eyes bugged. Something was wrong.

My throat was constricting. Something seemed to be pushing out from the inside, exerting enormous pressure on the base of my throat. I gagged.

"Caroline, are you choking?"

I couldn't find the energy to nod, but somehow he read my mind anyway.

"Don't worry, I'll help." He was forcing himself to remain—and sound—calm.

He limped over to me, wincing at every step. A huge pressure sat on my chest. My face turned red trying to force a breath. My throat was closed, my lungs pounded, and my brain raced with raving fear. As I fell unconscious, the terrible realization I was dying echoed in my sluggish mind.

So this is how it'll end. After all this — after the Indians, the sheriff, the terrible storms, Eli's fall, John's death, and Anne's cholera — I'll die choking on a piece of poisonous fruit.

The irony stung me perhaps more than the choking did.

My mind cleared back to reality as Eli whacked me on the back so hard I felt a bruise forming. The deceitful fruit flew out of my mouth and I collapsed on the ground, weak and gasping for air. I started to tear up as I crouched, trembling, on the floor of the caves. My arms gave out and I fell to the ground.

"Boo, are you okay?" Anne asked timidly.

I nodded weakly. I forced myself to take slow, deep breaths and close my eyes. The better to remain calm. The exhaustion of the day overtook my waning adrenaline. My last thought before I drifted into sleep was, *At least we're heading in the right direction. Tomorrow's the last day the Hydra has to live.*

The next morning the coolness of the tunnels woke me up. I sat up and shivered, peering around the dark, dank cave.

Eli snuggled closer to me, his teeth chattering. "Come back, Caroline. It's cold."

He didn't have to tell me. I rubbed my arms, trying to generate some warmth. The temperatures of underground in winter were less than toasty: the walls and the shriveled Hydra were coated with a thin sheet of ice. I brushed the ice off of the precious plant and touched the water in the stream next to us. I yanked out my freezing hand and took a quick moment to look around us. The movement triggered an intense pain at the base of my throat from my incident the night before. I massaged the spot, trying to alleviate some of the throbbing. Through the pain I shook my head. *At least I'm alive. Could have been even more poisonous.*

"You two," I said, ignoring the piercing in my throat, "we've got to get out of here. Now."

Eli sat up and blinked slowly, his tired eyes looking like they had to be forced open. "Okay," he said. He yawned and stretched, then stirred as he rose to his feet. He groaned and his knees buckled. In the midst of all the other problems, he had forgotten the sprain of yesterday. I ran to catch him.

"No, no, I'm fine," he protested as I came closer. He limped away, his white cheeks betraying his pain.

I scooped him up. He stopped objecting and snuggled in closer.

We walked along all morning without food. As much as I wanted to stop and get some of the pink fruit we passed, I knew from experience eating it would not help anyone. I tried to swallow my hunger and my thirst.

Then came the tree.

"Anne, do you see that up there?"

She leaned forward and squinted, straining to see something. She shook her head. "Nope," she said simply.

I wanted a second opinion. I glanced down at Eli, who was asleep in my arms. I rocked him in my arms to wake him up.

"Eli," I whispered, being quiet for his sleepiness, "do you see that? Off in the distance?"

He twisted halfway around and squinted, nodded, then snuggled back to his warm spot. Soon he was snoring again. I chuckled and kept walking.

I stepped on a sharp rock and felt a piercing pain explode in my foot and shock my ankle. I gasped and stumbled, setting Anne off balance and falling against the wall for a moment. With a conscious effort, I quieted my breath, ignored the pain, and kept walking. At this point the jagged pain was lost in all of the others which stabbed my raw feet at every step. I had to get out of this cave and get to Great's. If that meant a little pain in my feet, I would bite my lip, take a deep breath, and do what it takes.

I tried to remember where we fell into the cave, and which direction we were heading. By my calculations, we were headed in the general direction of Great's town. Still making good time. I smiled. We would need that time if we were going to get there before the Hydra died.

Soon we came upon the light spot I had seen. I squinted, my eyes unused to the bright light. I shaded my eyes with my hand and tried to look upwards towards the source of the light, my sight blinded by the sphere of light. It looked identical to the one we had fallen through, but had one important difference — there was a tree above us. The sides of the giant hole were covered with tree roots of all sizes and shapes. The hollow trunk of the tree covered the hole, so I could see all the way to the top of the old log. A hole in the side allowed the sunlight I had seen to pass through.

I checked my other surroundings. On my left, a dirt wall loomed far above me. Another dirt wall rose on my right.

About fifty feet in front of me was a hole in the ground which led to another tunnel—straight down. I set Eli on the ground. He woke up and yawned. "Nighttime already?" he asked sleepily.

"No... look up." I pointed to the wooden "roof" over our heads. "Oh!" He also shaded his eyes as he stared upwards. "What's the plan?"

"Simple! We'll just climb the tree roots and climb out the hole." I gestured towards the roots weaving throughout the dirt walls.

"Well..." he hesitated. "From my angle, at least, it doesn't look like the hole is big enough to crawl through, even for me."

I hastened over to his position and craned my neck for a view. I sighed. "You're right." I fell back onto my haunches. "Well, I guess there's nothing to do but try." I shrugged.

He nodded.

"I'll go first," I said. My shaky voice, weakened by the throbbing pangs of hunger, sounded very small in the lonely caves.

With a deep breath and a quick prayer, I laid hands on the thick root above me and pulled myself up. I climbed up until I was about twelve feet above the cave floor. My hands were sweaty as I leaned forward, very aware of the empty nothingness behind me. I tried not to think about it. Stepping on the thin root under me, I attempted to step on the next one up. But with a stomach-lurching crack, the thin one bearing my whole weight snapped. I dropped and was suspended by my hands.

I heard Eli gasp.

I dangled for a time before my kicking feet found a step on a thicker branch.

I realized I hadn't been breathing and I exhaled. I stood on the root for a moment before I moved on.

My trembling fingers touched the next branch and I pulled myself up. One by one, minute by minute, I made progress, slowly. It was slow going, but it was making a difference. I made sure to test every root before I put my weight on it. *Just in case*, I reassured myself. After what seemed an eternity, I made it to the top.

I stepped up on the next branch, intending to reach up.

I touched the dirt, intending to pull myself up.

My fingers touched slippery, liquidy mud instead of the solid dirt or roots I expected.

I slipped.

I fell back, screaming without realizing it.

I hit my head on a thick root on the way down, and I landed on my right ankle. Screaming pain shot up my entire leg, spreading throughout my body. I squeezed my teary eyes together and rocked back and forth, not speaking.

"Caroline?" Eli said. "I... I'm not sure how you fell, but it's alright. I'm going to help us get out of here. Don't worry."

I tried to open my eyes but couldn't for the pain. I heard a grunt, a stumbling movement, and then a silence. When the pain began to subside, I squeaked, "Eli?"

A voice came from above. "Yes?" it asked, tired.

My eyes shot open. I hoped he was not climbing. In the five minutes I sat on the cave floor, Eli climbed almost to the top of the hole. He reached for what I now knew to be mud.

"No!" I screamed.

He jumped, startled. The movement caused him to wobble on the branch holding him and I cried out. He regained his footing and held a different branch for support. I mopped my forehead, whispering a silent prayer of thanks.

"If I can't grab the dirt, how am I supposed to get up there?" he asked.

I grimaced. I knew what I had to do. "Hold on. I have a plan." I dragged my fiery ankle over to where the roots began and, with a breath of determination, began the painful trip again. My fragile foot pulsed with agony. I clumsily made my way up to the top. Even through my agony and clumsiness this time around took less time than the first because I knew Eli couldn't hold on for long. I came right up under him.

He looked down at me. "What are you going to do?"

"Get on my shoulders."

"But your ankle —"

I interrupted. "Never you mind about my ankle. Just... just get on my shoulders."

"But —"

"Just do it," I ordered, gritting my teeth.

He surrendered and put his feet on my shoulders, wincing in empathy.

The shock from my ankle as it took on the weight of another person was almost unbearable. It twined around my leg and shot up my torso, alerting my brain it was not prepared to hold me and was much less ready to hold two people. I ground my teeth and did my best to ignore it.

"Can... you reach... the top." I asked through clenched teeth.

He stretched, setting me off-balance. I grabbed a tighter hold on the root and prayed it wouldn't break. "No. Maybe another two feet."

I reached up, holding a bony root with a death grip. I hefted one foot at a time and with pain hoisted the two of us up. The renewed pain from putting my foot down again made me cry out. I was crying through my squeezed eyelids.

"Caroline," Eli said, looking down at me.

"Just do it!" I shrieked.

At least my foot's throbbing was now so intense I could no longer feel it. The only pain I felt came from the swelling.

"There, there, a little to the right...Got it!" he yelled. He grabbed the hole in the side of the tree and I lifted my shoulders to hoist him high enough to get over it. With a grunt and a groan, he tumbled out of the hole and out of my sight.

"Eli!" I called after about twenty seconds of silence. I wiped my watering eyes on my sleeve. Now that it was just me, the pain was not quite as bad. "What's out there?"

"Well," he started slowly. "You're not going to like this, Caroline."

Fear gripped the pit of my stomach. "Why?"

"I think it's better if you see. You wouldn't believe me if I told you."

His words rolled around in my brain. With the speed of a gunshot all of the horrible possibilities his words could contain flashed through my mind. Where were we? Or worse, what was there to greet us? Was there some kind of an animal to get us? Were we trapped in a canyon?

"Alright. I'm coming after Anne. Send me a vine to get her," I answered. The distress in my voice was clear.

After a moment Eli sent down a rope made of a long vine. Anne touched the end of it. "Anne, do you remember when Papa taught us how to make knots?" I said, still clinging to the side of the wall. I tried to sound sugar sweet so as to make the process easier.

She shrugged. "A little bit, Boo," she said.

I took a deep breath. I was going to have to coach her through this. "Okay, Anne," I started. "Take the end." She did so. "Put it behind you." She did. I sighed. My fingers were starting to tremble with my weight. "Okay, remember what Papa said? Put the end behind the loop. Alright, good job. Next I need you to tuck it in that little space there—see that? Yes, perfect. Good job. Now pull it as tight as you can, alright?" I whispered a silent prayer the toddler's knot would hold her for the twelve feet she had to travel straight up.

"Eli, pull!" I shouted. I saw her beginning to go up, and I prayed yet again. She passed right by me and up to the hole. Eli's arms reached inside and pulled her out. I released my pent-up breath.

"Okay, I'm coming!" I heaved myself up, tumbled through, and saw what was indeed unbelievable.

We had wasted one of the few days we had left, leaving us with the rest of the day to get all the way to Great's house. We were not even close to her house.

For in front of me was the forest containing the hole Eli had fallen into. We came out of the old, hollow Grandmother Tree against which I leaned when I suggested we go to the pond. I scoured my surroundings, frantic to find some small sign that what I saw was not true.

But it was.

About twenty feet in front of us was the hole where we had fallen. Still dangling off the boughs of the tree were the hard vines Eli had snapped off to make a walking stick. I groaned and held my head, much too confused to do anything else.

I felt months of anger, stress, and pressure which I had been trying to ignore seep throughout my veins, forcing its way out. I had to let it all go. Now was the time to use it. I looked up, the fire in my eyes flashing. "Come on," I ordered.

Without another ward I started speed-walking, my hair flaring out behind me and the younger ones' legs flashing back and forth to keep up with me.

"Caroline, wait... wait a second," he said breathlessly. He winced at the sting of his sprained ankle, though it had been bound well and Henry's leaves had taken away much of the pain. Anne loped alongside him as best she could.

"We can't. Not yet," I shot back. My ankle seemed like it was on fire, but the pain did nothing more than to fuel my anger. I put the extra energy into my speed.

"So... where are we going?"

"To Great's," I fired.

"What are you going to do?" he asked, trying not to direct my anger against himself.

I stopped and spun around. He jumped and skidded to avoid running into me. "You know what, Elijah? I'm sick of that question. And I don't want to hear it, not ever again." His eyes grew wide as I got in his face. "I'll answer you one last time, if nothing more than for the sake of finality." He nodded, his eyes wide with apprehension. "So here's the plan, and you'd better listen up because I'm not saying it again. We're going to get there, and we're going to get there in time to help Great-grandmother Pamela." I raised my eyebrows and stared at him for a minute. He nodded.

I let out a little more of my pent-up energy. I glanced back and saw Eli was getting out of breath from the speed I set for us. But we only have twenty-four hours to cover the remaining twenty-six miles.

"Hurry up," I said.

While we walked, or rather ran, I didn't hear a single complaint. They understood not to say anything to me right now. Not unless they wanted to be yelled at, anyway.

My mind was focused less on the burning pain of my foot than on the burning strain building up in my heart. The pressure, the fear, the grief which I felt fall on my own lonely shoulders took its toll. I reasoned it was a good time to use that stress.

Over my shoulder I saw Eli panting as he limped along, trying to carry the exhausted Anne on his back. My heart softened. I motioned him over and carried him on my back, then after a moment switched and took Anne.

In the next six hours we stopped once. After taking a quick sip from a stream and all but mutilating an apple, I yanked Eli and Anne to their feet and we were on our way again.

After eight hours of walking, I found my pace slowing. I was sweaty, tired, hungry, and my foot was beyond painful. I did not voice my main concern; today was the last day the plant was guaranteed to work. If we didn't make it to Great in the next several hours... I didn't even want to think of the consequences. It may survive an extra day, but there were no guarantees. No safety nets. This was the game of life, and there was life at stake.

Doubt filled my heart as I surveyed our situation. I wasn't sure how far we had gone, but it was not far enough. I motioned to Eli and the three of us went on.

As the evening fell and the moon beamed upon us, I carried Eli in my arms and still I walked. The thought of the approaching deadline spurred me on. I shuddered.

The moon went on its course and still my untiring pace continued. Still my numb feet continued moving, my eyelids falling and snapping open spasmodically.

I squinted as I looked to the skies. The sun was rising already. The last day of life for the plant, and if it died, then so did Great.

As the sun began to rise, I surveyed the sky. The heavens broke out into a wonderful halo of blues and yellows and pinks. The clouds came into view with a gorgeous crescent of pink flame. The sun sparkled and danced behind a wall of orange clouds.

I took a deep breath, grateful for the beautiful sunrise. Even if it was destined to be the last one on which Great could look with hope.

I looked ahead again. I was now depending upon what Mr. Lincoln had called "a day which is completely undependable." I had eighteen hours to get there. Total. No second chances. And if we didn't get there on time, then Great would die. If she died, we would be alone and friendless in the world, separated from all who might feel some obligation to take us in. I felt more of the weight of the moment fall onto my shoulders. I closed my eyes to block out the reality of it all, even if it was for but a moment.

I tripped on something hard and fell face-first on the ground. Eli tumbled out of my arms and fell to the ground next to me. He flipped on his side and went back to sleep. I remained on my side where I had fallen, too exhausted to get up. Though my conscience spurred me on to hurry, my body begged sleep. Even if just for a few minutes. I made a pact to myself; I would wake in no more than twenty minutes.

I woke up two hours later. Startled, I grabbed the plant, whose leaves were long past wilted and whose stem was already brown and droopy. In a panic I searched for some sign of life. I dug down about an inch into the dirt and groped the bulb. It was barely moist. Not shriveled, yet. I sighed with tense relief.

"Eli." I shook him. "Come on. We have to go now."

He blinked several times, unaccustomed to the light.

"Alright," he said. He cleared his throat and rubbed his eyes.

I felt a little jab in my eye, as if something had hit it. A piece of straw in the wind, or a bug. I rubbed my eye. I turned again. I felt the pain again. I blinked several times. That's when I saw the light reflecting off something buried in the ground.

"Eli, look!" I pointed to a shiny metal object. "What is that?" Judging by its placement, I guessed it was the thing over which I had tripped. I approached it.

It was an old metal axe. Its head was gleaming silver in odd contrast to its wooden handle. I picked it up, careful not to cut myself on the sharp head. Spinning it around, I found neither any defects nor any way to tell whose it was. I got a strange feeling this had been placed here on purpose, as if it was meant for me to pick up. I looked around and saw no houses from which it might have originated, no roads from where a traveler might have dropped it.

"It's like it came out of nowhere," Eli whispered, voicing my thoughts. "Maybe... maybe God left it here for us?"

I cleared my throat. "Well... if it is from Him, then we should take it," I said. He nodded. I handed the plant to him and shouldered the heavy axe.

We scuttled along all day, sometimes me carrying the axe over my shoulder, sometimes Eli dragging it behind him. We did not stop for a long time.

At about two o'clock, some solid object loomed in our horizon. I squinted.

"Eli, off in the distance—do you see that?"

He nodded. "Yeah, it looks like a sign," he said. "Can you read it?"

"No, I can't quite see it. Maybe another couple hundred feet." We pushed ahead a little.

He squinted and pushed his head out farther, straining to read the sign. I chuckled. *As if those couple inches will help him to —*

"Caroline!" he yelled. A smile grew on his face from ear to ear. He dropped the axe. Eli, who was always brave and strong, began to cry. "It says 'Springfield, Ohio, fifteen miles.'"

I dropped the axe and gasped.

We had made it! After all of our work, our sacrifices, our worry—it was almost over. The end was in sight!

My eyes were wide and teary and I shook with overwhelming joy. Anne screamed and ran towards me, grabbed my hands, and together we began jumping up and down. Eli joined in the revelry.

"Thank you, God!" I shouted towards the heavens.

"Yeah!" my siblings echoed. "We're so close!" I laughed. "We can do it!" "So let's go!" Anne cried.

I bent to retrieve the axe. I noticed it no longer felt heavy. Eli grabbed the undamaged plant and then we raced to complete our journey. No longer tired or discouraged, I found myself laughing for what seemed the first time in months. It feels good to be happy again.

In time our energy fizzled out. We now walked as our ecstatic vigor slowed to a frazzled meandering.

Around four o'clock, I felt a cold drop of water fall onto my head. I looked up and got another drop of water on the forehead. I wiped it off. Thunder rumbled in the distance, and the wind began to throw around my skirt and my hair. I shivered as a sudden wintry gust cut through my clothing.

"Caroline," Eli shouted over the thunder, "Let's go in there for a minute to escape the rain," he suggested. He pointed to a forested area.

We turned our course and began to head toward the dense forest. Lightning flashed in the distance and thunder rumbled across the sky. Our visibility grew smaller as the curtain of water dropped from the sky like a gigantic sheet.

We made a dash for the forest. The density of the trees made it almost like entering a building. Rarely did the pouring rain get into the dark and ancient copse. We grew silent as we entered the creepy forest. As illogical as it was, I found myself wondering if the gnarled and dark trees themselves might have ears. We approached a tree and a flock of agitated bats swooped over our heads, screeching. I jumped and looked over at Eli, laughing nervously. He chuckled in reply. Anne clung to my leg, her mouth agape. Lightning struck somewhere in the distance and the thunder responded, echoing in my ribs and shaking the trees. One of the trees creaked somewhere in the distance, a creepy shriek which sounded almost like speech. A branch as thick as my neck fell next to me. I screamed and dove away. Eli and Anne followed.

After a safe period, we crept back into the open, my heart thumping against my chest. I took a deep breath to calm myself and made a slow walk down the path.

I heard something above us. I shot a glance upwards but saw nothing but blackness.

"Eli," I whispered.

My words sounded screechy, foreign, and out-of-place against the raging sounds of the storm. Thunder rumbled behind us.

"Yes?" he responded in the same tone.

"D-did you hear something?"

"Well, m-maybe, Caroline, but I'm not sure," he stammered, licking his lips and shrugging.

I heard it again. It sounded like a growl. I searched for the source of the sound, but again saw nothing but blackness.

"Eli, Anne, let's get out of here…" I said through clenched teeth.

She let go of my leg and the two of them broke out into a run.

I believe it was their mistake.

The black panther jumped down from the high branch above us and started running towards them. His back legs hit me as he jumped, knocking me down.

Still dazed, I let out a scream. I rushed after them. The lightning flashed, lighting up the horrific scene, and the thunder rumbled. There was a sound of screaming, but I didn't know who it came from.

Eli was tired and could not outrun the beast. Neither could Anne. They were keeping ahead of him, but barely. I knew the big cat was playing a bizarre game of cat-and-mouse with my little siblings. They would not last long. I let out a desperate prayer this grotesque game would buy them the time they needed to escape.

I continued running after the pair, getting caught and slapped and bashed by branches and rocks. I felt no pain.

"Hurry!" I screamed.

I tripped over a giant log and twisted my already-sprained foot. I groaned with pain and fell to the ground, clutching it.

I had a moment of clarity as I realized I had to make a choice. I could walk out of here and save Great and myself, but Anne and Eli would die. Or, I could save Anne and Eli, but I would die doing it. There was no way to save us all.

I had to choose.

I stood to my feet and ran the other direction, as fast and as far as my feet could take me.

By now the panther and my siblings could not be seen. I had seen them veer to the right, so I ran straight, which was away from them. I stood up and whacked the cumbersome axe-head into a tree. There was no way I could run with it. Running like a madman and praying my lungs would hold out, I barreled away from the death-cat.

My lungs burned, screaming for breath. My stomach heaved as my legs went back and forth, back and forth. I cried as I ran. My memories hit me like the tree branches surrounding me on every side, a thousand images in one moment of time.

I thought of when our house burned down, and of who I was then. I thought of the look of destiny Papa had on his face as he died in my arms, of the trust John had in me when he asked me to get the flower for Great. I remembered Rachel, and Oliver when he tried to sacrifice himself to save us. I thought of Anne and Eli bravely giving their all to continue on our cross-country mission.

A roar and a bloodcurdling scream snapped me back to reality. I tried to ignore it as I ran faster. Soon they came into my view. Flashing through the trees, I could see them running like mad.

I kept running away. I was now perpendicular to the trio.

I stopped short and took a deep breath. The only way to get to them in time had been to cut them off as they ran in a circle. No way could I have run quick enough to catch up running behind them.

"Hey!" I shouted. I waved my arms above my head. "Over here, you stupid meat-eating kitten!"

Anne and Eli ran towards me, bringing death behind them. After a moment they ran past me.

"Keep running!" I shouted to them behind my shoulder. "Hey!" I shouted again at the panther.

I caught his attention. He stopped in the little circle of cleared trees and lay low to the ground, his tail switching. He growled.

I looked into the eyes of my executioner for a moment then ran off to the left, behind him. I heard him follow me.

The rain blinded me as I leapt over bushes, ducked under branches, swung over holes in the ground. I looked behind me once. He was close enough for me to see the glistening on his sharpened canines. I screamed and found the energy to add even more speed to my feet.

Lightning flashed in front of me, striking a tree that must have been a hundred feet tall. Both the panther and I stumbled backwards, our eyes reeling at the dazzling light. With a loud explosion, the wood splintered and the ground shook as the tree began to fall to the ground. It hit the ground with a quake and a series of echoes.

I backed away and felt something solid directly behind me. The tree. It closed me in.

I was blocked in by the panther, now. There were no climbing holds—no place left to run.

I tried to edge my way around the circle to avoid the tree. I kept my eyes on him.

I tripped over a root and fell backwards on my rear end. He bared his teeth and advanced towards me, emitting a deep, threatening growl. His tail switched back and forth. I watched as his claws shot out. I crawled backwards, wondering how it would feel to die. He snarled, pulled back his lips, and circled me. His padded paws thumped the ground in a drum-like beat of death, a song I was not destined to survive.

I backed into the tree and stood to my feet slowly, my hands touching the tree behind me. I would not die on my back, helpless. I took a deep breath. No, when I died, I was going to die like a hero.

As my hands felt around on the tree, I felt something.
The axe. This was the tree where I had left it.

I smiled. Now I had a chance.

I yanked out the axe and held it, prepared to strike.
Where Mama had failed to stp[the panther that killed her, I
would hit true.

I saw a large movement behind the panther, one I hadn't
counted on. It was Eli and Anne.

They had followed me.

They were coming closer.

My sacrifice was for nothing.

We were all going to die together, all from a black
panther, just the same as Mama and Papa.

My entire journey was worth nothing.

No, no! This can't be happening, Eli ran to the clearing as
silent as a mouse. He held a branch high over his head. He
seemed to be waiting for the right moment to bring it down
on the big cat. Anne was right behind him, holding a big
rock for the same purpose. Eli lifted the branch over his
head and prepared to swing.

"Eli, no!" I screamed.

My scream startled Eli and he stepped on a branch. With
a sharp snap, it cracked in half.

The panther swiveled around and saw Eli.

A gleam spread across the big cat's face and he advanced
toward the two. I screamed in terror.

The panther lunged at my face.

I slipped on the wet leaves in my hysteria and fell, my legs flying up in the air. He flew over my head and instead saw my legs where my head should be.

With a crunching sound I will never forget, the panther chomped down on my left leg, biting it off.

I screamed and he roared. His grotesque prize lay on the forest floor between his paws. I threw the axe in desperation, whispering a one-word prayer. *Please.*

By God's grace it landed in his back.

His roar stopped. He turned to me with bared teeth; as if he wished to see me dead.

He lifted himself off the ground.

I scooted backwards, whimpering.

He stopped mid-leap and collapsed; his teeth not five inches from my body.

He was dead.

Eli and Anne ran to me and hugged me so tight if felt as if they were breaking my ribs with the relief of those who have already lost a loved one and then found her again. They were both sobbing, as was I. We hugged each other, not willing to let go.

As my adrenaline levels took a dive, I turned aside and vomited at the sight, the smell, the pain of my leg. The river of pulsing blood stained the leaves around me cherry red, the bone obvious under the carnage had been my leg.

"Look away," Eli instructed. I complied. My head felt light. I saw blue spots swimming before my eyes, the reality of my surroundings fading away. I leaned back on the wet leaves, not even conscious enough to wonder what they were wet with. I heard Eli and Anne talking but their voices

sounded unreal and far away. I felt movement on the stump
of my leg but couldn't process it. I vomited again and
opened my eyes. Eli stood over me, shirtless. Anne stood
behind him, her face pale but determined. I glanced down
at my leg to see Eli placed a tourniquet on it with the only
thing he had left—the shirt off his back. I passed out.

The Stranger

I OPENED MY eyes and screamed. I tried to crawl backwards, but couldn't.

"Ssh, ssh, honey. I won't hurt you," soothed the lean woman standing over me.

I was hyperventilating from the sudden shock of waking with someone standing over me. I opened my mouth to shout at Eli and Anne to run. Keeping her eyes locked with mine, she crouched down and offered me a cup.

"Here you are," she said. She unleashed a small smile.

I was raspy and my entire body ached. I reached out and took it, suspicious but desperate. I grabbed the cup and looked inside; it looked like simple water. However, the past few months of kidnappings and frightening people was enough. I thrust it back.

"You take a drink first."

She obliged, gulping down a portion of the cool, flowing water. I licked my dry and cracking lips, tasting blood. I reached for the cup. As I glugged the water, splashing it on my face in my hurry to drink, she stood nearby and kept her respectful distance. Her hair appeared a greyish brown. She wore small gold hoops in her ears. Her brown and green eyes looked kind, but all the same, I wanted to be careful.

"Where did you come from, sweet pea?" I turned and eyed her suspiciously. "I just want to help you."

I was inclined to believe her. She gave us water and shelter. Her eyes reminded me of Papa, with the same gentle, loving qualities as hers. I finished the water and handed the cup back to her.

"At the risk of sounding rude, tell me who you are first."

"Alright: my name's Pamela Joyce Darley. Now," she smiled, "it's only fair you tell me who you are."

I let out a small gasp. My eyes teared up. I reached out and pulled her close to me, hugging her. "My name's Caroline Elizabeth Darley, and I believe I'm your great-granddaughter."

We hugged for a long time before we pulled apart and spoke at the same time. I caught up with someone I never knew but imagined for the past several months.

She stopped talking, and a light danced in her eyes. She laughed out loud. The sound hurt my ears. Her laugh sounded beautiful, thrilling, loud; a contagious laugh.

"Do I ever have a surprise for you," she whispered. She took my hand.

"Elijah! Dorothy Anne!" she called. Neither of them stirred, understandably exhausted from the day before.

I balked. "How did you know?"

She smiled revealing two large front teeth and one missing canine. Still the smile was delightful.

"Ssh," she whispered mysteriously. "You'll find out." She winked.

The two of us shook Eli awake. He wore an oversized shirt with red stripes on it. When Eli opened his eyes, he jumped backwards and yelled. Seeing me holding her hand, he edged towards her.

"Eli," I declared. I beamed as I swept out my hand. "This is Great."

He gasped, looking from me to her. His eyes were wide open, staring at me and asking me if it could be true. After all the trials and the sacrifices, was she standing in front of us?

I nodded, tears filling my eyes.

With a blissful shout, he catapulted off the haystack where he stood and landed at her feet. He hugged her ankles and scrunched his eyes closed. Tears of joy dripped down his nine-year-old face. She reached down and raised him to his feet.

"Hello, Elijah," she whispered, smiling.

Anne approached us with her beloved dolly in one arm. She hid behind my skirt and peered out at Great. I leaned down to her eye level and winked. "Anne," I said. "That's Great."

Her eyes widened and she looked to me disbelievingly. I nodded. She let out a tiny gasp. Great came around to my other side and made a tiny curtsey to Anne.

"Good to meet you, Princess Anne," she said. The corners of Anne's mouth turned up as she edged off of the back of my skirt the tiniest bit. "Lovely little girl you have there," Great said, gesturing towards her doll. "She's beautiful! How old is she?"

Anne looked at me, looked back at Great, and then smiled. She came out from behind me and reached for Great's hand.

"Come with me, all of you," Great announced, smiling.

We followed her out of the barn. I leaned on Eli to keep my balance. "So, where'd you get the shirt?" I joked.

He turned to me mischievous eyes. He grinned. "I kinda took it off the clothesline," he said.

I laughed.

We approached the house, a small white beauty with all sorts of flowers, from geraniums to nasturtiums to daisies to sunflowers.

The abundance of plants struck something in my memory. "Oh! The Hydra," I started, starting to limp back to the barn. I heard the door of the little house open behind me.

"Oh, yes! I'll explain later," she said. She and Anne went around back to go inside.

Eli trailed behind me.

I stopped alone at the front door as someone stepped out. I squinted as their face became more visible. It was someone familiar, someone I knew.

"Mama!!" I cried. I jumped over the front stair, one leg and all, and stumbled into her arms.

We wept and held each other, too overjoyed to speak and yet too overjoyed not to. My shoulder was wet with precious tears, tears from eyes I never thought I'd see again.

"B-but how?" I asked, sniffling.

"Well, it's a long story," she said. Her eyes sparkled with tears and ecstasy. She looked behind me, still grinning. "Where are the others?"

"Anne is already inside," I said. "Eli should be right behind us.

I pointed to the little boy rooted to the ground, his mouth and eyes wide open. There was a moment of stunned silence before, in one swift movement, she ran to him, flying over the front steps. She picked him up and whirled him around in her arms. The two of them yelled, crying, laughing, hugging.

"Caroline!" Anne shrieked from inside the house. My instinct kicked in. I ran to her without hesitation, my heart echoing with her shrill cry. I rounded two corners, limping because of my leg. When I reached her, she was being held by someone I never expected to see again.

Papa! He was crying on her shoulder, which he brought up to his level, rocking her in his arms. He squeezed and loved the little child, his eyes shimmering with tears. I stood in the doorway, paralyzed with joy.

He turned and his gaze fell upon me. His smile lit up the room. "Caroline!" he shouted.

"Papa? Can it be you?"

My last words were drowned out with a stifling bear-hug. I touched him, my eyes wide open. I put my head on his shoulder and breathed in the woodsy, clean scent of Papa. I wrapped my arms around him and cried. "Caroline," he whispered, "I never thought I'd see you again." He took my chin in his hand and brushed a hair out of my face. He smiled. "I'm so proud of you. You did perfect," he whispered. His eyes sparkled.

My heart almost burst with pride.

"Wait," he said. He frowned. "Your leg—"

I blushed. "It's a long story."

Great, who waited in the doorway, spoke up. "Everybody come into the kitchen and you can have some peanut butter cookies."

She offered her arm to me and I limped into the kitchen. Papa swung Anne onto his back and followed us into the kitchen.

Mama was panting as Papa, with Anne on his back, led Mama into a chair. He rubbed her stomach gently.

My jaw grew slack. "Mama! You're with child!"

She laughed as she massaged her protruding stomach. "I know."

I fell into my chair, a thousand thoughts running through my head. My mother was going to have a child — and by the looks of her stomach, maybe even twins!

I tried to clear my mind and move on to the story of their survival and journey. "Mama! How did all this happen? I saw you — you were dead!"

"Not quite dead!" I noticed she looked healthy as she laughed, her pink cheeks no longer scrawny and her eyes shining.

"So what happened?"

"Well, all I can say is God was with us. That's for sure." She smiled over her shoulder at Papa and he took her hand. "But as for the details, well…" she looked away, her smile falling. "There was a panther. He…" she took a deep breath. "He was nearby and smelled the blood from the rabbit your Pa caught. Then he saw it on your Pa's hands, and…" she shuddered and looked away.

Papa took her shoulders. "After that, you came in shouting and scared him off. Your Ma fainted, and I was floating in and out of consciousness. We were clawed up so bad…" he threw another understanding glance at Mama. "We thought that was the last time we would see you for sure." Mama nodded. Papa started gesturing with his hands. "Last I remembered, I was talking to you, and then I dropped into something like a catatonic state. I didn't wake up until three days later, when I was inside a house." He shook his head. "Well, it turns out a distant cousin of hers —"

"Mr. Mark Whitaker Izard, governor of Nebraska," Mama said with family pride.

"Yes — I was getting there," he replied in mock impatience. When he chuckled the smile on my face grew so big it almost fell off my face. He continued. "Anyway, your mother woke up before me and went to go look for help. The horse was gone, so she walked. When she got to a nearby town to find help, no one would talk to her except one old man — what was his name?"

Mama squeezed her eyes closed. After a moment she exclaimed "Mr. Dirksen!"

I jumped up. "Mr. Dirksen? Was he a cartographer?"

"Yes! He said he recognized us because of what you told him!"

"World of wonders!" I sighed, staring off in shock. It was a small world, after all.

Papa continued. "Anyway, Dirksen gave Mama directions to find the governor. When she got there, he recognized her from childhood and told her he would do whatever she needed to get help. They nursed me until I was healthy again. We stayed with him the shortest time we could — perhaps a week — until we were well enough to go. He was reluctant to let us go, but he understood. In fact, he gave us a horse and cart!"

Mama nodded, adding, "And every time we stopped in a town and asked about you, they said you just passed by! So we hurried on by, trying to catch up." She shrugged. "I guess some time we just passed you right by, because we made it all the way here, expecting to find you, and you weren't here yet!" She stood up and came around to us, then hugged our shoulders. "Oh, Caroline, Eli, Anne, I'm so glad we're together!"

I was relieved she hadn't asked about John yet. Either she assumed he was still outside or she suspected the truth and wasn't ready to hear it yet. I was glad either way, because I wasn't ready to tell her yet, either.

Mama sat back at the table. "How did *you* get here by yourselves?" she inquired.

From the sheriff to Henry to the Indians to the underground tunnels and to the panther, I related our tale of adventure.

My stomach rolled as I remembered Great's promise to tell me what happened with the Hydra. "What about the Hydra? Was… was it too late?" My last sentence came out in a whisper.

She shook her head. "I found it in your hands when you passed out. I knew what it was the moment I saw it." She came closer to me and took my hand, smiling. "If you arrived five hours later it would have been dead."

"But it wasn't? Too late, I mean?" I corrected, stumbling over my words in my hurry to get to the answer.

She shook her head and smiled again.

I let out a trembling sigh. It was all I could manage. *Hallelujah, we made it!*

Mama interrupted my exuberant thoughts. "And… what of John?" she asked under her breath.

My emotion drained away and came back in the form of tears. I took her hand. I felt a hard knot of remembrance in my throat as I broke the news. Mama's hand trembled. "Mama, Papa… I… I'm so sorry. We did all we could." An unbidden tear danced down my cheek. A bittersweet smile grew on my face. Mama's face was pale. "He… he died a hero, Mama," I said.

Mama buried her face in her hands, not saying a word. Papa stared straight ahead, his face set in a statuesque manner. His knuckles were bone-white as he gripped the edge of the chair.

Mama looked up with a groan welling up from deep within her. "Oh, it's time, Peter," she said, clutching her stomach. Great took her arm and led her into another room, whispering encouragements.

Papa jumped up and went to put on some boiling water. Eli, Anne and I sat together, unwatched, at the table.

I took a breath and idled up to the closed door of the bedroom. I knocked. "Mama?" I called softly.

I heard a groan in response. I took that as permission to enter and shut the door behind me.

I took a quick look around the room. I turned to Great. "What can I do?"

Several hours after I went in, a shriek echoed throughout the few rooms in the small house. Then the shriek mingled with those of two small and brand-new ones.

The newborn twins were red-faced and screaming, but cute and precious nonetheless. My eyes widened as I saw something amazing; after I lost John, I gained two more siblings—both brothers.

The next week, a flurry of decisions were made. We were planning a celebration for Great's disease cure. And then there was another celebration for the birth of the twins, who survived their early births but were beautiful, healthy, and growing like weeds. They also, without question, possessed the loudest pair of lungs I've ever heard. Especially at four o'clock in the morning, when I was trying to sleep.

The day before the big celebrations, I jumped out of bed and tied back my hair, tiptoeing out of the house. I smiled as I took deep breaths of the cool, refreshing morning air. This would be the perfect day to play pirates with Eli and Anne later. I rolled out the sticky dough, still lost in thought of all the times we played our favorite make-believe game together. John made one of the best pirates. I smiled wistfully.

A voice spoke behind me, making me gasp and drop the rolling pin. It was Papa.

"Good mornin'!" he whispered, greeting me cheerfully.

"Papa, it's not nice to scare people!" I teased, still a little scared from his jolt.

"Oh, I just thought I'd come help you with breakfast. Plus," he added, "I thought you might like to help soothe the babies."

He handed over the twins, David and Jonathan. I thought the names fit perfectly. The Biblical friends—and John's first and middle names. It was perfect.

"Well, me mateys…" I said in my best pirate voice. I stared into their peaceful, beautiful faces. My gaze traveled up into the sunset as it crowned the sky in a host of heavenly colors. "Looks like I've finally found *real* treasure."

CPSIA information can be obtained
at www.ICGtesting.com
Printed in the USA
FSHW022010240220
67507FS

9 781733 709323